In That Heaven There Should Be A Place for Me

STORIES OF THE MOHAWK VALLEY

James Buechler

Cranberry Books
Duxbury, Massachusetts

Copyright © 1994 by James E. Buechler

All rights reserved. No part of this book may be used or reproduced without written permission except for brief quotations in reviews or articles.

ISBN 0-9639437-0-7
Library of Congress Catalog Card Number: 93-74562

Cover: "Six O'Clock" by Charles Burchfield. Watercolour on paper. Jennie Dickson Buck Fund, Everson Museum of Art, Syracuse, N.Y. Reproduced by permission of the Everson Museum of Art.

Published by   Cranberry Books
P. O. Box 1229
Duxbury, MA 02331

Printed by Rogers Print Inc., Plymouth, Massachusetts

Contents

Foreword   1

The Second Best Girl   3

In That Heaven   25

The Paper Boy's Last Day   57

The Ambulance Driver   71

Pepicelli   91

John Sobieski Runs   117

The Proud Suitor   151

On Cuthbert Street   179

Magister Pietro   211

The Washing Machine   231

Foreword

While the stories in this book are all set in the Mohawk valley of upstate New York, the characters and the dramatic situations described are imaginary and have no real existence whatsoever. The stories were written, and some of them published, over a long period of years and it might be said that the life represented in them no longer exists either. It is a life that is always evoked for me by Charles Burchfield's 1936 watercolor, "Six O'Clock," reproduced on the cover with the kind permission of the Everson Museum of Art, Syracuse, N.Y. Six o'clock was the supper hour in the high gabled houses of the area, set together in rows like the ones in Burchfield's painting.

The people living in these houses were a mixture of the children of recent European immigrants and the descendants of the English and Dutch who had settled in the area originally, all brought together by the General Electric and American Locomotive companies, established around the turn of the century. In general the Europeans were gathered in the city while the country was the territory of the older inhabitants. But the life involved a movement between country and city, city and country, and the culture (as we say now) represented by each, that is reflected in the stories.

> The farmhouse lingers, though averse to square
> With the new city street it has to wear
> A number in.

My own family lived for ten years in a farmhouse become a city two-family in a Burchfield-style row of houses, though the street, which bore the farmer's name, had been squared to the house rather than run through arbitrarily as in the poem. And I remember well the passion for "a new house" or "a house of our own" that followed on the Second World War and resulted in the city's further extending itself into the country.

The earliest of the stories, "Pepicelli," was first published in *The Harvard Advocate* and later received an O. Henry Award. "John Sobieski Runs" and "The Ambulance Driver" first appeared in *The Saturday Evening Post.* "The Proud Suitor" was published in *Mademoiselle* and reprinted in *The House of Fiction*, edited by Caroline Gordon and Allen Tate. "The Second Best Girl" appeared in *Redbook* and was reprinted in the O. Henry Awards volume. All of these stories have been altered more or less for this collection.

I want to emphasize that the names used for characters do not refer to any persons living or deceased within living memory. John Sobieski, for example, is the name of the historical King of Poland who led his army south to break the siege of Vienna by the Turks in 1683. The name was chosen for these associations.

J.B.

The Second Best Girl

The Second Best Girl

All during her high school years Shirley was in love with Tom Vinciguerra, the football hero.

Tom didn't even know she was alive. She wasn't a cheerleader or anything like that. Her marks were good, but even in her marks she wasn't "somebody." She was always just below the leaders, the bright ones who edited the yearbook or were in the plays or went off to college afterward on scholarships. It seemed unfair to her that she should fall just short in everything, and it made her work very hard. Gradually she raised herself to twelfth in her class. At commencement the first twelve were called forward together, before all the others. The superintendent of schools presented their diplomas while the principal stood by, smiling. He spoke to them all by name. When only Shirley was left he appeared slightly surprised, he couldn't think who she was, but he nodded to her and said, "Congratulations."

She was in love with Tom Vinciguerra — there is no use asking why. These unobtrusive, hardworking, well-behaved girls are attracted just as much as the opposite kind to the type of boy, often enough wild and reckless, who possesses already the strength and appearance of manhood. It is such boys who are likely to be involved in accidents with automobiles, or in trouble with the police, or in getting some girl pregnant. But such things weren't enough to frighten away Shirley, quiet as she looked. She saw plenty of them at the city hospital, where she worked after school. Her trouble was that Tom just didn't know her. So she loved him from a distance. She realized she had no chance.

She did have another boy, who was not so far away from her. He had grown up in a house four blocks from her own, whereas she never saw Tom except in the highly charged, cosmopolitan atmosphere of the big city high school. One night in late November, when she was fourteen, Will Schuler had asked if he could walk her home after choir rehearsal, which let out at nine o'clock. The choir had already begun practicing for Christmas midnight Mass. Will had grown quite tall all of a sudden; he sang bass. Shirley was wearing a red parka; she had on red boots, and a white kerchief tied under her chin. On a small, midblock street bordered by long backyards, Will pulled her along, his large bare hand tightly clasping her mittened one, to behind a dark garage where the owner threw his old lumber. There Will sat on a box and Shirley sat on his long knee, which swayed at first with her weight, and she let him kiss her many times. Within its white binding her cold, smooth face, touched by Will's face, was alive with amusement and happiness. The wind blew around the garage, but they were sheltered behind it. Afterward when she was home, upstairs in the warm house (she lived on the second floor of a two-family house), her cheek felt a little sore where the collar of Will's big lumberjack shirt had rubbed against it. Even her lips felt slightly chapped, which made her smile.

After that she liked Will Schuler. They were both fourteen years old. Several more times they stopped in the same place after choir rehearsals. On a cold clear night near Christmas they made their way out to the garage over deep glowing snow covered with a hard crust. It broke with a punch at every step. Will sat down, crumbling the snow that capped his box. Shirley shivered and laughed — he might at least have cleaned it off. She liked Will, and she knew Will liked her, because at Christmas he gave her a little present. He had even wrapped it, in white paper and seals, though there was no card. He gave it to her saying, "Here — this is for you," while they were climbing the steps to the choir loft just before midnight Mass.

After the Mass, however, though it was another cold bright night, with the same hard and glowing snow spread over the ground like water around the dark shapes of the houses, Will had to go home with his family in their car. The Schulers opened their presents together after midnight Mass and then slept late on Christmas morning. So Shirley had to walk along the little street to her own house by herself. In a way she didn't mind being alone. It was a night in her life when she was happy, what with Christmas and the package that Will had given her. As she walked over the hard-packed snow of the road, with patent-leather shoes and new chilling nylon stockings inside her boots, she could think that at the same time, not very far away, across a distance of only three or four streets, downstairs in a house she knew from the outside very well, there was Will, who liked her. She supposed vaguely that someday she might be married to Will, but it wasn't anything she could picture to herself — as, for example, living with him somewhere, upstairs or downstairs in a two-family house. She went home and had something to eat and then slept late herself on Christmas morning.

Before going to bed, though, she unwrapped Will's present. He had given her a fat little diary, the kind you can buy at the ten-cent store, that can be locked shut with a key. The first things she wrote in it were about herself and Will.

After Christmas she never saw so much of Will again. Now that there was nothing in particular to practice for, he came to choir only rarely. He walked her home those nights that he came. For herself, she still liked Will, but she saw that Christmastime, when she had been so happy thinking of what had only begun, had really been the high point of her happiness with him, which she wasn't likely to reach ever again. In June it was she who had to ask Will if he would take her to the graduation dance at the junior high school. She couldn't afford to be bashful. Will accepted. It was the first formal dance she had gone to.

That summer she worked long days in the hospital (she had always wanted to be a nurse) and saved her money. She usually worked weekends, and she didn't know what Will was doing. Probably he worked, too — or he might have gone away somewhere. But in the fall he turned up the very first morning on the school bus that carried them both to begin tenth grade at the imposing new high school in another part of town.

In high school her life changed at once. The place was so large. There were so many people coming from all over. Some of them were important, were doing things. She felt quite alone and abandoned to herself. Everyone she knew, from her own part of the city, seemed to dissolve away among all these other strange people. Later on some of them rose into view again as they became important; the others seemed lost forever. The great school upset her, yet it attracted and excited her. She wanted badly to have a part in it, but she couldn't seem to find a place, somehow. All during her three years she seemed only to stand aside and watch what was going on. She couldn't mingle with the leading people, though she admired them and wished she were like them. She did what she was told, she made good marks, but she had no flair. In her last year, when her first cousin, who lived across town, entered the school,

10 The Second Best Girl

Shirley watched her become somebody almost immediately. Soon more people knew Trish than knew her.

"Trish — what's wrong with me?" she asked once.

Trish, tiny and lively, a cheerleader already, paused and thought. "I don't know.....there isn't anything wrong with you. You do everything you should." She laughed mischievously. "Maybe you're too good."

The words struck Shirley, so that she lost heart. "I don't want to be good. I want to be the same as everybody else. How should I start being different?" she pleaded. "You know. Tell me."

"Oh, I don't know!" The younger girl broke off, exasperated. She understood very well, what Shirley was asking. She knew that she was different from her cousin. But she had her own life. Her success exhilarated and preoccupied her. She had to work very hard at it. She was doing a million things — she had no time. In a few years she went off to college, left the town altogether. She never came back afterward except to visit.

At the high school Tom Vinciguerra burst on Shirley's awareness all at once. For her he was the excitement and danger and chance of the whole place — a medium-sized, somewhat brooding, heavy-set boy, very thick within his clothes. He would sit in the back of the classroom watching the teacher with a steady, unafraid look. He was the best football player the city had had in many years. Week after week during Shirley's first autumn the newspapers carried his name and ran pictures

The Second Best Girl 11

of him. The school had never been good at football before. Now they won almost every game, and Tom Vinciguerra was doing it virtually by himself. He was talked about everywhere in the city. That winter the chamber of commerce chose him as the Athlete of the Year — which meant something, because the city also had someone on the Olympic speed-skating team and a successful racing car driver. But Tom was more important. He received a trophy, and his picture appeared in the papers once more.

Shirley was working every Saturday, but on Thanksgiving she finally could go to a game. She had never seen one. In the strange football clothes with the high, hunching shoulders and the big black shoes Tom looked much bigger than he did in life. His round white helmet looked like the top of a bottle, to her. His suit was red underneath it; he looked like a ketchup bottle. She saw the dark ball come flying back to him, he waddled forward clumsily, just shoving people ahead of him as though he wanted to get through a door a little faster than everybody else. So many players crowded around him that eventually he fell down. It didn't make much sense to her, it was all so clumsy and confused, but she saw that it was serious. What convinced her of that was the faces of the players in the other colors when they were close enough to see. Some of them looked quite old. They were dirty and tired. She watched them as they bent down at the beginning of each play and put their heads up and waited for Tom Vinciguerra.

12 The Second Best Girl

They wanted badly to stop Tom, but they couldn't. He did what he wanted with them.

Tom continued to be famous all his and Shirley's three years. Every year he was in at least one class with her, but she could never say she knew him.

She grew more reserved. She didn't smile easily. She went around with an unpleasant, long-faced, horsey expression. Early in her senior year, when someone turned to her with new interest and asked, "Oh! You mean Trish is your cousin?" she softened immediately and her looks themselves abruptly improved, for she was fond of Trish. "Yes," she smiled. "Didn't you know that?" But she was asked the same question too often. In the end it only made her more long-faced and unpleasant than ever.

Then something unexpected happened. Will Schuler invited her to the senior ball, which was held the weekend before graduation. Though Will rode on the same school bus, Shirley had not thought about him for years. She accepted because she wanted to go.

They could have made a good couple. Will was tall and fair, though his skin was blemished. Some girls might have thought him good-looking and attractive otherwise, too. In the morning he was filled with life, the wit among the boys who sat at the back of the bus, but once at school he put on a pair of small ridiculous glasses, blinked, looked stupidly serious, and guffawed in a vacuous way with his friends in the halls after lunch.

Now, however, in a powder-blue dinner jacket, he was really handsome. They got out of the taxi and walked up to the columned entrance to the school; the walk was lined with onlookers — curious people who lived in nearby houses, younger students, some few seniors not going to the dance. Will bent his head; he was self-conscious and so was she. She was thinking she might well take to him again. They entered the vast gymnasium, decorated beyond recognition, its backboards and climbing ropes all hoisted into the dark upper regions of the ceiling. And then, for most of the night, they simply sat at a little-disguised card table with a lighted candle on it and watched the sweep of the long dresses and the matching scissors of black trousers of the dancers at the center.

For high school had infected Will, too. With a clumsy inarticulateness he brought out his confusion and admiration. "There's Geordie (a well-known girl). Who's that with her? Some college guy?" "There's your cousin Trish — how do you like that, she's only in the tenth grade." "There's Vinciguerra, I'd hate to get in that guy's way. You know they're going to pay *him*, to go to college?"

He talked freely, though he was usually tongue-tied at school. In his own way he was pleased to be there. Finally, while they were dancing, he said to her, "You know, I'm really glad I came with you, though, instead."

Shirley drew back her head and shoulders to look

at him while she danced. "Why are you glad about that, Will?" she asked.

He drew closer. "Ah, you know," he said with unendurable confidence. "I never have to worry about you, what you're going to think."

He meant it. He was grateful to her. He was overcome by his own feelings.

"Not like some of these characters here," he added moodily, gazing toward the center of the floor.

Shirley said nothing. She didn't even ask him what he had meant when he said "instead."

The week after graduation she heard that Will had enlisted in the Navy. But she was too busy moving into the student nurses' quarters next to the hospital to think much about it.

Not many people are more cut off from the rest of the world than girls in an old-style nursing school. They live under a rigid discipline administered by stern, highly starched older women. They work hard on the floors, study fat difficult textbooks and get two weeks off each year.

In this place Shirley flourished. They knew all about her beforehand. She was the sort of girl for them — she was not playing. On the floors she was capable and managing even as a student. Mainly, she never flinched. She endured all the whining uncertainty of sick people without pity, for she knew she was in the right. She was held up as a model to the frivolous, who didn't like her for it. But she was always professionally cheerful.

After getting her R.N. she went home to live with her parents. She took a bus to the hospital every day. Some of her old friends thought she had grown unpleasantly hard. "That's the way it is with nurses. They get used to bossing people. Oh well. They have to be that way."

At two o'clock in the morning the state police brought in three men from a crossroads to the north known as the Four Corners. Out there was a big sagging wooden tavern left over from better days in the 1920s. According to the owner five men, who were together, had been huddling and talking in loud confusion before they left the place, evidently making some sort of plans. Suddenly they pushed outdoors and got into two cars. The cars backed and cut and ran around the ramshackle building once in opposite directions, crossed, came out each on a different road and then rushed into the intersection, where they demolished one another. Two of the men were crushed instantly. One died on the way in, but the last two were still alive by morning.

Both had been wearing miraculous medals. A priest coming in early to make his visits went to them first. He gave extreme unction to one and then carefully moved his black case and his oils to the bedside of the other.

This man had lain through the night with his

eyes open, never quite surrendering consciousness. He had watched the wide-hatted state troopers, the young interns and the nurse who had worked over him downstairs. He remembered their bringing him up and settling him in this room and leaving him. It is never fully dark in a hospital. The sounds came down to him of the night nurses talking, desultory and indifferent, at their desk at the center of the hall. Now he watched the perfunctory ministrations of the priest over the shape in the white bedclothes across the room. But when the stout black-clothed man, eyes tired and circled, still preoccupied with the articles necessary to his task, moved across to him, he went wild. He twisted his upper body powerfully — he had an enormous chest and shoulders, accentuated by the bulk of the dressings — and cried out and swore at the indifference and perfunctoriness that would carry on with things when he himself was in such straits; though he would never plead for pity from that indifference either. It was Tom Vinciguerra, grown five years older.

Alarmed, the priest drew back. A male attendant hurried in to hold Tom; a doctor came and gave him something. He had spent himself anyway.

When he awoke it was morning again. The daylight fell across the bed opposite, which was flat and freshly made.

"That one went out last night," said a nurse quietly to another as both stood outside the

The Second Best Girl

doorway and looked into the room.

"How about this one?"

"Oh, we could lose him, too."

Tom's eyes looked toward the doorway with a furious uncompromising hatred, but the two women had already gone down the hall. He could hear a rattle and movement of things on wheels out there. A weak, steamy, coffee tinge reached him; they were serving breakfast.

During the day he lay and watched. Sleep had done him some good. But though he was awake he would not speak, or take notice of anyone who came into the room. The little aide who came around so cheerfully with a fresh water carafe shrugged and went out. He resisted anyone who tried to do anything for him — except the doctors. They had seen resentful patients before and paid no attention to him. They put his limbs where they wanted them, and if he resisted, they were firmer and it hurt excruciatingly. They paid no attention to that either. But everyone else Tom fought off. Late in the afternoon a nurse who was to give him a needle went out to the desk and complained.

"Oh, he is!" declared, far out there, the nurse in charge.

And she came in swiftly with a smooth but tight-lipped, long-faced expression, trailed by the other. With a quick little movement she seized Tom's wrist, which lay along the sheet. She was young, she wasn't large, she held him only with thumb and forefinger, but the circlet they made was like cold metal. The grip pressed the sharp edges of the bone inside the flesh and actually hurt. All he could do, in his surprise, was to watch her other hand as, holding the needle lightly like a dart, she threw it into the slack flesh of his upper arm. The fluid was pumped home, the wrist released at once. The first nurse nodded and was satisfied. The two women went out and Tom was left alone, wondering and afraid at his weakness.

They treated him like a child. But he was a child; he had no strength. He was afraid. Let them do what they wanted with him. He grew apathetic. He slept a great deal. And he began to recover. Before long he was hungry for meals. It took several days, but he grew settled, and even contented, in the hospital routine. Though he said little, he cooperated. He was happy in the solitary, most simple way, just to be alive.

As for Shirley, it might be thought that now she had Tom Vinciguerra delivered to her in this way she would be thrilled. It wasn't so, however. It had been eight years since the first, greatest excitement of her attraction to him, and she had come to earth long since. There was nothing very wonderful about his coming — people she knew were continually passing through the hospital. Tom's fame was so old that it meant nothing now. Somebody mentioned that he had never finished college, had never even played on the college team, having been injured soon after his arrival. He looked much heavier.

She treated him as he needed to be treated, as though he were no different from anybody else. But from his bed, with the studious eyes of the football player at the back of the classroom, Tom followed her comings and goings. He saw that she was hard and managed the place. It was something he could appreciate, because for all his size and strength he had never been simply a "natural athlete"; he knew that nothing much was ever accomplished against the painful physical obstacles of life without the grimmest purpose. It was the secret of his success — many boys had been as big as he. Though he dealt in violence he had never been reckless until, failing, he had returned to his home city.

One morning Shirley had washed his back and was giving it a rub. "Do you remember me?" he asked her. His voice was uncertain and sounded as though he had a cold.

"Yes. You went to school with me — me and my cousin Trish."

He was silent, thinking. "Was Trish your cousin?" he asked her meekly, but surprised.

Shirley laughed and expanded as she had the first time the question was asked of her. "Yes — didn't you know that?" For she still thought of Trish with admiration. She was proud of her cousin. "Trish is out in California," she told him. "She's got another year of college, but she's married already. Her husband is going to be a lawyer."

Tom shifted his hips and settled down so that he could see her. "They have good football teams out there....I think. They're on television." She was gathering up soap, cloth and ointment. It was quite early, before breakfast, a gray and quiet time in the room. Shirley emptied and rinsed his basin. As she did so her face, momentarily thoughtful of her cousin, appeared in softer, more affectionate, more diffident lines. It was the only time Tom Vinciguerra saw her like that in all the weeks he was at the hospital. But his mood of convalescent happiness made him think the best of everyone, and it was the only face he remembered of her once he got out.

After a while he called her up and came to see her. Shirley treated him coldly. He had no job now. In her own work she was quite successful. It really seemed she could hope for something better. But though she was hard and balky with him, Tom always treated her as though she were some tender beauty. When girls had sought him out in his good days he had never bothered long with any of them; he would not compromise his fame. Now he thought very little of himself and was quite afraid of her.

Shirley did want to drive though, so she allowed him to teach her. Driving was absolutely new to her; her father had no car. She was much too hesitant, and failed the road test.

That same night after supper Tom drove her out into the country to a field reached by sandy wheel tracks

The Second Best Girl 21

and enclosed by birch and pine woods. "Now drive," he told her grimly.

Fearfully she changed gears, but sitting close to her he crushed her right foot with his own heavy left one. The car (one he had borrowed) jumped forward and bounded over the dry hard tussocks of orchard grass, smashed down the heads of high goldenrod, ran underneath its charging hood the stalk of a little midfield birch. Inside, they bounced up and down and when Shirley pulled her foot from under Tom's he pressed even harder on the unprotected pedal. His brooding eyes looked outward, straight at the jumping, oncoming trees. Shirley jumped on the brake with all her might, and the vehicle slowed — but kept going. Tom pressed relentlessly; the car would break out again. She jumped on the clutch and they stopped, but the engine wound up and shook as though it would burst. They moved again. She pulled on the wheel. The car jumped and ran, the trees scraping its side. There was no way out. She did nothing but try to stop for she didn't know how long. Tom pressed and Shirley tried to stop. His big hand covered the ignition. Shirley perspired and shouted aloud. She finally got the trick of keeping the car in low gear and turning within the confines of the field. It occurred to her to steer between the trees along the road they had come in by. Tom kept the accelerator down even when they were out on the paved highway — but Shirley held the car under control. Her excitement was up. Though trembling, she laughed in her access to

The Second Best Girl

power. Then at last Tom relented. She allowed the car to slow down, guided it off the pavement, and stopped. "There — now you can drive," he said. She turned and hugged him wholeheartedly.

And so they were married. They lived in a flat just down the street from the hospital, and Tom went back and forth every day to the state teacher's college. Everybody remarked how Shirley had come out. In two years Tom had finished, and was hired as football coach at their old high school. He was very successful. He and Shirley went to the school dances as chaperones. Everybody knew who she was — she was the wife of Mr. Vinciguerra, the football coach.

One morning when she was spending the day at her mother's (she was pregnant and had given up nursing), Will Schuler telephoned.

He talked in a way she had never heard from him before. He had acquired a line, a loud mixture of nervousness and stupid self-esteem that she felt painfully he must really be ashamed to utter. He spoke of his doings in the Navy, stationed here, stationed there, and so on. When he got around to asking about herself she said only, "Well, I'm married now, Will."

There was a pause, and he asked in the same assertive style, "Yeah? Who's the lucky guy?"

For some reason Shirley found it difficult to answer. "You remember Tom Vinciguerra?" she said with some embarrassment. "He's the football coach at school now," she added, as though to mitigate something.

All the rest of the day she felt bad. She sat through the afternoon in her mother's house and waited for Tom to pick her up. It was football season; he would be late. The baby was expected near Christmas.

Not that she wasn't happy. After all, she had got what she wanted. But only after Will called did she think about it that way. And it didn't seem to her the same thing, as getting what you wanted. It made her feel better, somehow, to think that the joys of her life had come without her asking for them; she hadn't even recognized them when they came. Perhaps she wouldn't have been able to bear them otherwise.

In That Heaven

In That Heaven

When Gus Klein moved into the city from the village across the river, where he had lived the first ten years of his life, he found everything strange.

There were more houses around. They were packed closer together and their porches came out almost to the sidewalk so that, as he walked between the lines of them, over several streets to his new school, he had the feeling they were watching him. He felt exposed. There were new kids, some of them menaced him, and he had no idea who he could fight and who he could not, as he had known — and everybody else had known — in the village. And all around loomed the two-family houses, dark and forbidding at their windows, icicles hanging at their sides, with a terrible icy wind whipping down the tunnels of the long streets and a perpetual gray sky between the rows of roofs overhead.

Gus understood they had moved to be closer to

the G.E. Works where both his parents went every day, his father early in the morning until suppertime, his mother just before he got home from school until midnight. Gus could hardly imagine anybody working so late, and it was a wonder to him to see his mother up in the morning before he was, afterward. He had a little sister and an older brother; but his sister was always with the four little kids downstairs, and his brother disappeared on a bus for the high school at the same time in the morning as his father did, and got home at night even later.

And hardly had they moved to this new place when the boy began to feel strange, sharp pains in his stomach. Sometimes the pains were in one place, sometimes in another. They came when he breathed. He might stand up, after just sitting awhile, and they would be there. He carried around with him constantly the fear that he had appendicitis, but he was terribly afraid of an operation and never told anybody about the pains; and this made him still more afraid — at any moment he might "really get it," his appendix would rupture and he would die. But after several weeks, though the pains were as bad as ever, he hadn't died, and so on balance he was less afraid of them than of the hospital and he said nothing.

From the bay window at the front of the house where he sat in the late afternoon over homework,

In That Heaven

Gus caught sight of his father turning the corner. Quickly the boy threw on his mackinaw, pulled on his overshoes and without stopping to buckle them hurried downstairs and turned up the street. His father was still a bent, distant figure in a long gray overcoat, coming along slowly with little mincing steps.

Gus ran the first short block. He turned down another bleak long street ending in still another, which he followed to the first corner.

The corner house was a two-family made of red brick. At one side it had a turret capped by a pointed slate roof, making a round room upstairs and down. Gus went around back and entered the lower flat without knocking.

A plain-looking young woman, the boy's aunt, was doing her washing in the dark kitchen. Her damp hair was half coming down from the top of her head where she had tied it up out of the way, and she wore a big black button-up sweater to keep warm. The house was stove heated. Everything smelled of wet. The air was steamy from contact with the broad surface of near-boiling water in a galvanized washtub sitting up on the coal range. Dirty clothes lay piled on the wet linoleum. In the middle of the floor the washer itself worked with a furious splash and twist inside, its cover firmly on, the motor underneath humming loud and ominous, the machine with every stroke moving a little on its casters. Though busy at the wringers his aunt called over the noise, "How are you, Gussie?" but she couldn't stop; and the boy walked in his overshoes over the mound of dirty clothes, through the field of intense heat thrown out by the range, and into the farther rooms.

Gus went through to the round room made by the turret — in this house, a music room. He pulled a string, and the light bulb overhead came on. There was a player piano and all around, under the windows, orange crates standing on end as bookcases, packed with the narrow brown boxes containing piano rolls.

He mounted a roll in the piano, loosened his mackinaw, kicked off his overshoes, and began to pump the pedals. Black and white, the keys jumped up and down. Loud music came from inside the instrument. The boy swayed from side to side as his effort shifted from one leg to the other. In a strong soprano voice he sang out the words that trickled down, one by one, at the edge of the dashed and slotted paper in its movement from roll to roll.

> *There's a star-spangled banner waving somewhere*
> *In a distant land so many miles away.*
> *Only Uncle Sam's great he-roes get to go there —*
> *There I wish that I could also go some day.*

In the song a crippled mountain boy wanted very much to be fighting in the War, but could not be; and some similar longing, some urgent feeling that he did not really belong where he was but somewhere else, combined with an utter hopelessness that he ever would be in such a place, was in Gus's voice as he sang the closing line:

In that heaven there should be a place for me.

Even so he had to laugh as he sang "1942 Turkey in the Straw" — the old square dance tune with new and funny words about Hitler and Mussolini. He sang "American Patrol" and then "Dear Hitler I Wrote You a Letter." But instead of "The Modern Cannonball," about the shells that were going to fall on Germany and Japan, Gus sang "The Wabash Cannonball." He just liked thinking about a train that crossed the whole country. After that he sang "Red Wing" and some others.

His aunt had cleared up in the kitchen, now all yellow with light, but was out on the back porch hanging her clothes. It seemed a funny time to be doing it, to Gus; his mother washed every Monday morning without fail. "Where's Norman?" he asked her as she came in. He liked it that with this aunt and uncle you could call them by their first names.

The young woman came straight to the stove, her face shining, her nose running a little. Her hands were red from the wet clothes and she motioned as though washing them in the heat that rose up, the boy fancied he could actually see it, from the dry radiant stove top.

"Overtime, I guess." The heat fixed her gaze as an open fire will. "Every night this week, so far."

Gus had taken the chair beside the stove and tilted it back to the wall. He lay there in the heat until his clothes on that side began to burn his skin; then he shielded himself with his mackinaw, catching the heat with it against the moment he would have to go outdoors.

Warmed somewhat, his aunt looked at him. She was his mother's sister, but seemed scarcely older than his brother Leo.

"How are you, Gussie? I see you going by to school in the morning. How do you like it here now?"

The boy's eyebrows drew down. "I hate it in the city," he said. "When I get older I'm going out in the country to live."

His aunt, still half-absorbed by the warmth of the stove, said vaguely, "Well, you'll get used to it. When we were little, your mother and all of us, we lived pretty far out."

Gus still frowned, thinking. His aunt blinked, and roused herself. "Stop in here anytime," she told him. "I like people to come and see me."

The rubber of Gus's overshoes had begun to stink with heat. He pulled them on, though the buckles were almost too hot to touch. He got into the heat-saturated mackinaw, zipped tight the hood, shoved his hands deep inside the breast pockets, and went outside.

Half the way home he was warm, the other half

In That Heaven

he was cold. It was dark already. The wind rushed through the streets and eddied in the narrow spaces between houses, and yet the bare trees remained motionless in the cold.

Up in his own house too the kitchen was ablaze with light, though the rest of the flat was thick with shadow. Gus could hear thumping down below, and kids squealing. He felt hunger in the pit of his stomach and higher up on the right, just at the lowest rib, a little knot of pain.

"Hi ya," said his father cheerfully.

The globe of the overhead light was reflected twice in Mr. Klein's glasses as he sat in what was already, in this new house, "his" chair. His graying hair was carefully combed, but mussed in one spot. His white collar was unbuttoned and his necktie had been pushed to the side, though tucked into a dark buttoned-up vest with a silver watch-chain strung across it. One elbow rested on the table and two long fingers, pointing straight up, held delicately a burning cigarette. Beside the elbow on the oilcloth stood a brown quart bottle half full, and on the cabinet shelf behind, an empty one. Mr. Klein held in his other hand a jelly glass of froth and amber liquid, and by the way his lower lip protruded, betraying an indecent pink inner wetness, his son knew he was talkative already.

"Where's Leo?"

"Not home yet." Mr. Klein exhaled smoke from his mouth and nostrils, adding to the cloud in which he sat. "Nobody home yet, jus' me."

"When are we going to eat?" asked Gus, while his fingers pressed his lowest rib.

"Not going to eat. The Republicans, they won't let us eat anymore." Mr. Klein poured beer into his glass. Gus looked at the folded-over newspaper falling from his father's lap. "Once this War is over, they'll put us right back where belong. Be against the law, to eat. Yuk!" His lower lip extended, and he drank. Gus laughed in spite of himself.

"Guess I'll make an egg then," he said.

Gus went out to the ice box on the back porch. He found two full beer bottles shoved up against the food, made a face and said to himself, imitating his mother, "Tsk!" Back inside, he flung bacon into his pan, wrenched on the gas, saw the blue flame pop on, and waited. The bacon began to melt and float, then smell, then crackle. Gus broke in two eggs.

"Say," called his father, "throw in a couple eggs for me, will ya? I could use some salt with this stuff."

The boy pinched his lips together, but he broke in two more eggs. He pushed the smoking yellow egg-pieces here and there with a wooden spoon and divided them finally onto two plates and pushed one across to his father. Mr. Klein tamped out his cigarette while Gus poured himself coffee. He shoved his father a fork, and salt. Himself, he used ketchup and some bread.

"They thought they would fix him," Mr. Klein jeered, and his lower lip pushed out, his speech became intentionally thicker, "with this slick fella with the *mustache*. They been crying ever since he went in there and started doing things fer the people, fer a change. Boo-hoo. Rights o' property. Ya dassn't take my money away from *me*."

Gus scarcely listened. He didn't care about the Republicans, as long as they never got elected; for if they did, his mother had once said to him seriously, "We'll all be out on the street, selling apples."

He cleaned up the dishes and went back to his homework but his father went on for a long time about "the Almighty Dollar," "the Little Fella," some people he called "the Big Bugs," and every so often, with a thick, ironical pronunciation, "Mister Doo-ey. Do 'ee or don't 'ee? 'Ee don't, and 'ee never will!"

Gus's little sister came upstairs saying she had eaten down below, and went to bed. Later his brother Leo, dark-haired and silent, wearing glasses, came home from his job downtown. He went straight to bed. Gus followed. He covered up well against the cold in his place at the foot of the broad bed. He had found that if he drew his knees up, lying on his side, the pains wouldn't bother him.

Once in the night he woke up. He could tell by the sour smell filling the room, and by the mountain of covers on the other side from him, that his father had come in. The man lay growling into his pillow. All at once he pronounced distinctly, "Yuk!"

When it happened again Leo, from his iron cot

by the window, called out, "Shut up, for Christ's sake."

Then Gus covered his head and slept. In the morning when his mother pushed open the door to wake him and smelled the sour smell filling the room her face twitched, and at breakfast — his father and Leo had left already — she asked him in a tired voice, "Well...how's things?"

"All right," said Gus.

At the right time he would set out in the gray and white morning for his school. Sometimes he wouldn't come straight home, but would stop at the house with the turret to sing with the piano. If he stayed long enough he might be there when his uncle Norman came in.

Norman was taller than anyone else connected with the family. He had narrow shoulders, but large strong bones. In winter he wore a mackinaw like Gus's own, and a red hunting cap with earlaps. His eyes were large and lively and mobile, his mouth shaped like the letter V ("V for victory," Gus thought when he had first noticed it), his expression, even when he was silent, a grin of some kind.

Norman worked at the American Locomotive Company, where they were building tanks for the War. Coming home he would sit down at the kitchen table and drink off in quick glassfuls a quart of orange soda. There was always some for Gus, too. On his back porch

Norman kept whole cases of soda, mostly orange and root beer. He owned guns and hunted, but the guns were kept at his mother's place in the country and Gus's own mother had been careful to keep him and Leo away from them.

Gus didn't mind. His true joys, in his old life, had been swimming and fishing. Late the previous summer he had finally mastered water, he had swum the Mohawk River, and he was afraid, now in this long dark season, that he was "losing it." He loved to fish. His life across the river in the village had been happy. When he turned nine he had said to himself, "Now that I'm nine I'm glad I'm not eight any more, but I wouldn't mind being nine all the rest of my life." When he turned ten it was the same. But then, in the fall, they had moved.

Gus had gone fishing with his uncle Norman once or twice. Now as they drank orange soda together in the winter evenings they talked of shiners, wall-eyes, black bass, lakes and creeks, and Gus's mind was filled with sunlight and heavy trees and the wonderful brown opacity of water, always mysterious, the unknown quarter of the world from which you might expect anything.

Still, there were strange things about Norman. His laugh was a kind of giggle. When his lips opened to make a double V, his teeth were almost green. Gus's mother and the other women could become very angry with him. "Isn't he terrible," his wife would have to apologize. "That wasn't a nice thing to say." When Gus's aunt first brought him to visit, just after they were married, he had even said, "Nobody goes to church in my house. Sunday morning I turn the key in the door and put it in my pocket." He giggled and looked around, his eyes white and lively. The women were silent with embarrassment; the children, Gus included, stared at the man.

When finally Gus got home his father would be talking, usually about Roosevelt and the Republicans. Sometimes his brother was there, and then the two would talk more soberly. Leo would be going into the army at the end of the summer. Gus didn't even listen. He agreed with them if it came to that, but he hated the talk. He loved President Roosevelt. The words "President" and "Roosevelt" meant exactly the same thing to him, and he thrilled whenever he heard the high silvery voice on the radio.

Meanwhile the days were changing. The air was warmer, the sky farther away, the upper branches of the high maple trees rose-tinted in the afternoon. The cinder-crusted snow had shrunk to glazed piles on drab lawns and in lots. Down on the river the ice had broken up, collected in jams and then moved out, leaving great caverned blocks here and there along the banks. The suckers were spawning in the brown turbulent creeks tributary to the Mohawk.

They began to fish.

"You have to hold your face straight," Norman said to him.

Meanwhile Norman's slender rod was bucking and arching under some enormous strain. The round leading-eye dipped and retreated in jerky, live jabbing motions as if the rod were standing on its own handle and striking at the water like some thin, vicious snake. Sitting knees high, Norman leaned back a little and wound in. His reel made no sound. Eventually he stood up, his rod became a straight thing pointing down into the dark water that stirred and roiled itself now, yet without actually breaking, and there came up out of it along the tilted surface of the rock two forms, twitching and black — out of the river and onto the dry portion of stone at Norman's feet.

"What's that — two of them?" Gus asked.

His uncle stood up very high — dark and solid, looming — against the clear and glowing sky. From where he sat on his own rock slab Gus watched him wind the two fish in. When they were lifted clear the bend of the rod was incredible, nothing so slender should bear such a weight. The heavy and torpid suckers hung without moving. One, hooked through the belly, dangled crosswise and showed red fins against the white flesh.

"Look, will you," the boy complained. "There's one that was just swimming by, not even looking at his bait — and he catches it when he pulls up for a bite on his other hook. I don't even get a nibble to see whether I *could* catch one or not."

"You don't hold your face straight," Norman told him, and giggled.

The shelves of rock were a foot thick and slanted down, ten or twelve feet long, into the water. A great many of them had been laid against the open soil of a cut bank where the creek mouth opened into the river. Now Norman climbed the angle of his slab and from its end stepped to the river bank's top, where a cornfield began.

In the second week of April the field was not yet ploughed. Gus's aunt was sitting up there on a car blanket. She looked strange because she was wearing the wide-shouldered jacket from a man's dark suit and her real arms, clothed in a light-colored sweater, came out from under the top fastened button and seemed like an extra pair. Under the spreading jacket she was wide and large — though her neck was so thin as to show the veins and cords, and her fragile head appeared incongruous upon so large and grave a body, fixed to the earth against the blanket by its own gravity. She was heavy and pregnant. She was reading a folded over magazine in the failing light that made her square page the lightest thing in all the darkening land and water around.

She glanced at Norman as he squatted to take off his fish. Eight whitish bellies lay stiffening in the grass already.

"Gee — isn't that a lot in one night."

Norman grinned faintly. The brightness of his eye expressed cheerfulness, satisfaction, complete well-being. He let himself back down onto the rock.

"I must be too far up the creek, or something,"

Gus said irritably. "Yours must go way out into the river."

Norman baited up and cast out. "Told you," he said. "You don't hold your face straight."

The boy had sat in the same attitude for an hour and a half. His rod was propped across a broken rock, and he hugged his knees and stared with absolutely intent eyes at the spot where his limp fishline pierced the smooth plane of the water. After that it ran down into the water-filled trough of the creek that in turn gave way to the greater trough in which the heavy and brown Mohawk slid past, making swirls at its edges, carrying drift with a speed calculable even to the eye. Gus couldn't see a thing down there. He was sitting only a few feet from his uncle, whose line dropped into the surface too, running out in the same direction, yet Norman had already pulled in ten fish while no twitch, no sudden stiffening of the line, would show in all that time that anything down in that dark region where neither could see was paying the slightest attention to his bait. He had reeled in and baited again. He had cast out in different places. Nothing would touch his worm. Gus lost himself. Then there was only the wide brown water coming down, the flat bank of the opposite shore, the three great black humps of the Rotterdam hills behind them like camels, the glowing white sky; with nobody speaking, his aunt up on the bank behind him and his uncle, all three of them motionless with their faces turned up river toward the final weak dazzle of the yellow sun, that had already dropped down.

In That Heaven

It was curious how they sat immobile, facing the same direction as though it were the region of hope. And so it was. The woman's burden grew each day, its weight drew her closer to the earth and the man along with her. The two waited, expectant and patient, knowing there was nothing they could do for themselves. But the boy seethed. Their calm did not extend to him. His hope was wilder, and the more unsatisfied. He had had his own calm formerly, when it had not so much mattered how things turned out — because he hadn't thought about the end of things, they were going on forever.

No sound came from off the dark river hurtling down, except just once the wash against the prow of a long tanker, one of the first of the season, plowing toward the Great Lakes. But the wind coming down with the water was cold.

The boy Gus came to himself. He thought he saw his black line dancing out and he seized his rod in two hands and whipped it back over his head — but it came easily, nothing pulled against him, and when he reeled up he found his worm unmolested.

"God damn it!" he cried in a fury. His fingers pinched the soft crawler from the hook and flung it, in three pale pieces, out on the water. Nearby the tall man giggled.

"You don't hold your face straight."

"I hold my face as straight as you!"

"Don't keep saying that," his aunt's voice called

down. "He wants to catch a fish in the worst way. He can't help it if he isn't lucky. — Don't worry, Gussie," she said to the boy, "we never caught this many in one night either. You can have some of Norman's to take home. Nobody will know the difference."

"I don't want any of his," said Gus in a voice that came straight from his hot throat. "I'm just as good at fishing as he is."

"Except he doesn't hold his face straight."

"Don't say that," his aunt pleaded.

"You shut up!" the boy shouted. "You damned ignorant farmer! You're so ignorant, you stink. Just because that's all you ever do, is go fishing. Just because that's all you know anything about."

Norman's eye came white and alive, his lips pulled back exposing his teeth. "Ignorant farmer?" He giggled.

"Nobody else eats suckers. Nobody else eats anything out of this filthy river."

"Oh well," his aunt interposed, "we always wash them good first."

Gus strung a fresh nightcrawler. It was so dark that when he cast he couldn't see the swing of sinker, line and worm but only noted by the splash the spot far out where they landed and sank. He sat down and clenched his jaws and hugged his knees. He couldn't see his line at all, but he held it delicately between his thumb and forefinger. But nothing troubled it; nothing would help him.

His uncle stood up again. Something had rushed out with his line as hard and strong as a machine. For a long time Norman worked the rod and reel. At last he brought out a carp with shiny criss-cross scales, twenty inches long. With the heel of his work shoe he crushed the creature's head. Then he turned and flung it as hard as he could so that it flew, a black thing passing high over the young woman, and landed in the cornfield beyond her.

"There — why don't you eat that carp. You eat the suckers."

"Oh, nobody eats carp," his aunt called down.

Norman giggled. "The Jews eat carp. Let Gussie take it and sell it to the Jews. Gussie, they give you good money for a carp."

"Shut up. You're not supposed to talk like that. Jews are just as good as you are."

"Sure, they're just as good as me. Their President, he was just as good as me, too. Nowhere near as good as me any more though — is he."

"He wasn't just their President. He was everybody's President."

"We'll wish we had Dewey in there now, boy."

"No we won't. Nobody wants him."

"Gets us mixed up in the god-dam War. You work day and night and you still can't buy nothing."

"You're so stupid! If it wasn't for him you wouldn't even have a job."

"Reel up."

Standing, both brought in their lines. One bright star, and another one near it, were out already above the river. They stripped their hooks and drove the barbs into their rods' cork handles. Up on the bank Gus's aunt waited with the blanket folded over her arms. Norman picked up a whitish bundle, the newspaper in which she had wrapped the fish. Gus lifted the fishing box by its handle and they started along the creek under bare squat willow trees throwing up new shoots like hair.

"That Norman is so ignorant," said Gus as he entered the yellow kitchen. "Christ, how I hate him."

The room was the same as ever — overheated, smoke-filled in layers like heavy webs, his father sitting there in necktie and vest. Except that Mr. Klein's eyeglasses lay on the oilcloth, fragile ear-hooks bent askew, and without them his father's forehead seemed larger, his gray-white eyes tiny and deep within damp sockets, looking tired and sick as they did sometimes when he slept late on weekends.

"Yeah, he never knew much."

"You know what he did tonight? He stopped at a gas station and filled his tank right to the top, and when I asked him how he could do that with the rationing, he just giggled. That isn't right. And then he talks about the Jews, and President Roosevelt — just because he's dead."

Trembling, the boy sat down in a chair by the

stove; he suddenly felt like crying himself. His father turned his head to the window, saying vaguely, "Yeah."

"What's the matter with that guy? Didn't he ever go to school? He says everything you shouldn't say. He does everything you're not supposed to do. What did President Roosevelt ever do to him?"

Mr. Klein's heavy head swung slowly from the window. His eyes studied the lower buttons on his vest. "Those people never think," he said, scarcely paying attention.

For some time they both sat. Gus finally thought about President Roosevelt, that he really was dead, it had been on the radio, people were talking about it already before he had gone fishing. Suddenly, in a kind of panic, he asked his father, "What's going to happen?"

"Nothing."

"Will we lose the War? Will you and Ma lose your jobs?"

His father sat hunched over. "Maybe we'll lose 'em, once the War is over," he said without looking up.

Gus sat and tried to concentrate. But he couldn't keep Norman out of his mind. "God," he said aloud after a while, "how I hate that guy!"

He hated his uncle. No matter what you said, his father at least knew what was right. Gus even took a new way to school that would not take him past the brick house with the turret.

But one morning in late spring his mother said to him, "You know Helen has had her baby. Why don't you go and see her sometime?"

"Why should I?"

His mother, looking tired, not eating herself, shrugged — it was none of her business; though, Gus knew, she had given up her sleep to go over there in the morning lately. "Oh, women get blue, you know, when they come home from the hospital. With nobody there all day."

Gus missed the player piano. So he stopped off in the afternoon, but very early.

He found the house strangely still, lit by white gleams of sunlight thrown in through the narrow windows. His aunt sat on the sofa with the baby, a blue and white cloth package partially unwrapped, lying in the crook of one arm.

Helen looked terribly white and terribly thin. The white breast that she kept with guiding fingers securely upon the baby's mouth, though like a soft and shapeless bag it would roll around unexpectedly, appeared so fat and swelling as scarcely to belong to her.

"Hello, Gussie — How're you?" she said.

But all the time she looked only at the baby's little head, about the size of a cat's head with sparse moist-looking fur, with a peculiar absorbed little smile. Gus sat down and talked to his aunt, but she didn't listen so he stopped. It was so quiet. Once he heard the baby take in its breath, a sigh like an old man's. Gus sat and watched for a while but then felt he shouldn't, for some reason. From his chair he could see the crowded disarray of unfamiliar things, mainly white and blue cloth articles, in the sunlit music room. There would be no singing in there now. Bored, he looked around and saw that the flat was more all-apart than ever — clothes in a pile on the dining room table, things on the floor, three of Norman's big shoes dropped like stepping-stones toward a dark bedroom doorway — unlike the strict neatness of his own house. And the sum of it all, the boredom, the messy rooms, his wild and cruel uncle, his aunt's strange ignorance of these things and even happiness with them, dispirited the boy suddenly and drove him outside into the bright street where he said to himself, "They just don't know how to live."

When school had closed for the summer there was nothing for Gus to do. Everything he loved was so far away, he did not know his way to it.

In the morning, downstairs on the empty front porch, he thundered in a big wooden rocker and sang the words to every song he had learned from the player piano. By the time he had run through them all the sun was high. His mother came out with her pocketbook on her wrist and walked down the street toward the stores. Upstairs the telephone rang.

"Norman is moving things out to our new house today," his aunt told him. "You know, on the hill, up the Hollow Road. Maybe you'd want to ride out with him. You could get off at the creek and go swimming. Is your mother there?"

"No."

"He has to come back here, and then he'll be taking another load after supper and he could pick you up. He's rented a truck. Should I tell him to stop?"

"Yes," said Gus.

The back of the truck, its load lashed secure under dirty mover's quilts, hunched up behind the cab like the final swollen section of a summer insect. Everything the vehicle did it did only with the greatest strain and difficulty. Norman's feet in their big shoes jumped time and again on the worn pedals, and let them bang-out. His large awake eyes moved from the windshield to the mirrors to the load behind and when he would call, "Anything on that side?" he meant for the boy to take it seriously and Gus, holding to the doorhandle and saying nothing otherwise, would stick his head out and bring it in again and call back, "All right!"

Even outside the city they moved with great labor. In the distance Gus made out the deep level green-yellow thickness of the cornfield, hardly separable into rows, and the line of paler bushy willow-heads marking the creek and the way to the river. His uncle stopped, and he got down. The truck strained and whined and lumbered off the concrete to enter a dirt road opposite.

Gus swam through the long afternoon. He moved out on the brown lukewarm surface for great distances over the depth below. Each time he returned to shore he would be well down from where he had started, and he would pick his way back again over the rocks. The long slabs were now all exposed, the cornfield bank higher; the river water carried particles of matter and was never clear. Fish broke the surface all through the day. Once Gus hauled himself onto a big red channel buoy. He looked across to the distinct, dredged-up stones on the far bank, but he saw no reason for swimming over there. He swam again. He watched the barges move by. He lay on a rock slab and listened to the metallic bang, and then the transferred shock along the line as a locomotive began to move a string of cars across the river, out of his sight. He swam again.

There was nothing to do anymore. He had eaten his food a long time ago. He was tired of proving he could swim every ten minutes. There was no place he wanted to swim to.

A soft muffled detonation shook the air a great way off — to the west, beyond a gray haze out of which the smooth river poured down. The thickening haze dissolved, all at once, the white sun, and a sudden nearer blast jolted the surrounding air, the rocks, and even the flat-surfaced river.

The boy looked up apprehensively. He put on his clothes and hurried under the willow trees. At the highway he sat up on the bridge railing and looked toward the city. He knew it must be after supper. The day was not only suddenly dark but extraordinarily quiet too, empty of both sound and motion. In the stillness he was aware of the slightest isolated movement out among the black cornleaves that sprouted cascading from stiff frothy-top stalks. Up the highway to the west, the round poplar leaves on one side only of a great tree twirled individually, and were still. From up the river came new explosions, accompanied by a shaking of the black landscape, low after-rumbles, and, against a deep sooty sky like locomotive smoke fallen between the hills, broad flickerings and white jabbing lines like those in radio tubes. He heard a curious twittering sound of birds, such as he had heard only a few times before, when he had waked up and it was still dark though he knew, perhaps from the birds, that it must be morning.

With the storm's darkness began to mix the ordinary lowering of approaching night. The few cars began to show yellow headlights. Gus crossed the highway to the Hollow Road. He shivered. The air was in its first stirrings, its first flowing and pouring, turning suddenly cold. He was in mortal fear to be standing under trees. He looked toward the city and squeezed together his hands. Just then the tidal wave of wind that advances before the rushing front of rain swept down the valley and over him. Every part of every living thing bowed and shook, the trees showed the undersides of leaves and seemed they would be stripped bare, though the foliage mostly drew in protectively, like a bird's feathers; the corn ran waves; branches broke from the stiff willows; and as he watched the charging air the truck

In That Heaven

hood, wearing its case of dirty tin, suddenly placed one wheel on the concrete beside him. His uncle Norman stuck his head out the driver's window and called around the windshield.

"Get in!"

Gus climbed up and pulled shut the tin door. He was in a little cabin of quiet while things continued to writhe in the blast outside. The truck, with its roped canvas-covered hump behind, began to whine and crawl up through the twisting hollow. A wave of clear water broke over the three glass surfaces of the cab and continued to pour over them. In a moment the water was rushing downhill over the stones of the road as over a creek bed, swiftly turning brown. The truck ground on. Norman said nothing — he had all he could do to drive and see.

As they came out of the woods on the first of the road's summits, with a level before them and fields on both sides, the storm's electrical wave struck. With an awful slow tearing something opened the protective dome of the world overhead, and the jagged rent admitted a white light five times brighter than the ordinary light of day. Driving sheets of rain could be seen for miles around; every wild tree and line of hill, everything in the lower distances, the broad quicksilver river and every individual delicate girder in the railroad bridge, was as sharp as the heads upon the grass stems in the field beside the road. Then a mountain fell on the truck, miraculously without crushing it, bounced, and boomed on down the valley.

    Gus clung to his doorhandle — but it was of metal, so he let it go. He turned on his side and rolled into a ball and shut fast his eyes, but the flash was as bright as ever from a fresh split directly overhead, and a new thunderous blast welled up from the ground underneath. Then things outside were stilled, for the briefest instant — long enough for him to discover that the truck had stopped moving, the engine had stalled, they were trapped in this high place in the open and his uncle, while grinding the weary starter, was cursing and taking God's name in vain.

    The boy waited to be scalded to death by some white, wet flame. He was afraid and at the same time terribly sorry for himself. Like most children he had already thought, long before this, that he might die, and he could imagine nothing more terrible than that he, himself, should be imprisoned in a coffin, unable to get out, and buried in the ground. All around him the lightning flashed, inescapable. The sounds were of cracking and rending, the thunder's terrible pounding, the regular pour of water over the cab with renewed slashing and drumming as wave after wave drove into them from the west.

    Gus opened an eye. He saw his uncle Norman — the railroader's cap, the long nose, the Adam's apple hard as a stone — sitting quietly at the steering wheel. Once the man reached and cleaned a patch of windshield with the back of an enormous hand. When he saw the boy looking his head turned, his eye brightened, his lips drew back in the old grin. He giggled quietly.

The boy's eyes watched him. Norman turned and cleaned his side window, and gazed out. The rain was at its loudest and brightest, it was all silver, there was so much of it as to be nearly solid. Gus sat up. He cleaned the window on his own side. In the continuous lightning he could see water rushing not only on the road underneath their truck, but downhill in temporary streams through the fields.

Between flashes it would fall black-dark. Now the rain fell straight down upon the cab and hood. When at last it slackened, though flickers and rumbles still came from the edges all around, Norman turned a switch. Small instrument circles suddenly glowed. The running and liquid road, with rain still falling into it, was lit up before them. Norman got out; Gus could hear the pop and rumble of bending tin out there.

His uncle's face thrust into the cab. "What've you got on?" He looked over the boy's jersey and dungarees. "There, let me have that." Gus handed him his rolled-up swimming towel.

When Norman climbed back in again Gus asked, in a voice that sounded strange to himself, "What did you do?"

"Wiped her. She got wet, that's all."

The man's big shoe pressed the starter. The engine ground and ground and then caught, with as grate-

In That Heaven

ful a sound to man as the warmth of fire is a feeling. The heavy truck wheels bearing Gus Klein and his uncle Norman rolled slowly up the road once more, turning aside the water that ran down and broke against them.

Because it was dark and late, Norman drove to his mother's farm beyond the woods at the top of the hill. He was looking after things while his mother, and his two brothers, fished at their camp in the north. Gus had been to the farm before, it was where they found nightcrawlers, in the manure among the matted golden stalks of straw. But he had never been inside the weathered house.

It was very rough, he thought. There were guns mounted above the doorways. Deer heads thrust out from the walls, their mild eyes fixed upon distance. The glassy-eyed feathered bodies of owls and pheasants stood or roosted on dark furniture pieces. This house, too, had a player piano.

But Gus went outdoors with his uncle to the waiting animals. Afterward Norman made a wood fire in the kitchen stove and Gus scrambled eggs with bacon in a black iron frying pan. He went to sleep in a bed upstairs without sheets.

Sometime in the night Gus woke up. The rain had stopped. In the faraway unfamiliar room he was calm as he had not been calm in almost a year. He felt older. He thought that when he got back to the city he would try to find something to do, something he could make money at. He felt immensely older. He thought he would be getting older very quickly now. Not to be an old man, or even as old as his uncle Norman, right away; but he thought he would hardly be the same, from now on, two days in a row.

The Paper Boy's Last Day

The Paper Boy's Last Day

"Answer, why don't you, for Christ's sake!"

"Why don't we just go to the front door?"

"Because — the bell never works. After a while you know all the bells that don't work, and you go around to the back right away. You can always tell — the button wobbles when you push it."

Once again the older boy, the taller of the two by a head, smashed his knuckles hard against the wood of the door panel, causing the glass panes above to rattle.

"Come on," he demanded in a low voice, fierce and threatening, "I see your light on in there."

The tall boy stooped a little to peer inside. His breath clouded on the cold glass. Immediately within was a dark hallway, and then a darkened kitchen, but yellow light from a bedroom halfway through the house fell across a heavy dining room table. Beyond was the darkened living room with gray opaque windows looking out on the street.

The shorter boy, wearing a heavy mackinaw with

the hood up, stood by patiently. There wasn't much else he could do. The broad straps of two full newspaper bags crisscrossed upon his breast and back like the cartridge belts of a Mexican bandit. He was such a wide figure, with the thick and square-looking bags on either hip, that in climbing the stairs he had had to shift one bundle in front and one up behind him — hunching under the one, stumbling upward into the other; and now their two weights combined to pin him, nicely balanced, to one spot on the upstairs back porch floor.

A woman appeared all at once in the dusky hallway and pulled the old door quickly inward.

"Paper," snapped the boy who had rapped. "Sixty cents this time."

Warm interior air came rushing out of the suddenly opened house, smelling sharply of beer and fried onions on top of numerous long-accumulated, indefinable smells. The woman was short and rather fat and wore a light-colored robe of smooth material. She had long dark hair, which was tied behind her back. Her flesh and skin seemed very white and soft. "Didn't I pay you for it last week?" she asked in a soft and young voice.

"I came Friday night and Saturday morning and Saturday night, and nobody answered," said the boy who had been knocking, bitterly.

"Who is it, Honey?" came now a man's voice, high and thin, on the warm strange-smelling air.

"It's the paper, Joey!" the woman called back.

The Paper Boy's Last Day

"Here — C'mere!"

The young woman turned, leaving the door still ajar. Watched by the two boys, she went back and disappeared into the doorway of yellow light. They waited together outside on the upstairs back porch. A cold wind blew across the long backyards from alleyways between the high two-family houses on the next street over. Yellow lights were on in the kitchens over there, indicating that supper must be going on within. The backyards were quite dark, the air dark and smoky in between; but overhead the sky was still glowing and luminous, for it was early spring and no longer full dark at suppertime.

When the woman came back she handed the tall boy a limp and moist dollar bill. "You can keep the change," she said in her soft voice.

Smartly the boy's punch rang out, two loud snaps upon her subscriber's card. "Thank-you-very-much-Mrs. Greco," he announced, businesslike. His purse rang shut; the door closed softly.

Out in the street again it looked as though nobody were home in the house upstairs.

"If you didn't know any better," said the tall boy, "you'd go right by. You wouldn't even bother trying."

"Forty cents," said the one laden with newspaper bags. "That's twenty cents apiece."

"What are you talking about?" demanded the other as they began to walk. "That's my forty cents. I'm just teaching you the route. You don't know how lucky you are. By rights you ought to help me two weeks, instead of just the one. And anybody that doesn't pay up by tomorrow morning, you'll have to give me the money when you get it from 'em next week. I'll figure out how much you owe me — I'll come to your house."

"I forgot to give her her paper."

"Throw it up on the porch."

The boy in the mackinaw whipped out a fresh dry newspaper, from which the loose cuttings still hung. He tried folding it into a six-inch square, but stiff and quite heavy, it resisted.

"Thirty-two pages," remarked the other. "Gimme."

The tall boy appeared only to slap the paper two or three times against his chest. Next moment the square white disk flew upward, with sharp corners spinning, and dropped on the upstairs porch.

"How many can you fold in a minute, Summers?" the short boy asked.

"I can fold twelve, when they're eighteen. Eight or nine, when they're twenty-four. You remember the day the War ended? Sixty-four pages, Jesus! I left half of 'em out on the corner while I did the rest in two bags. Then I went back for two more bags. And they didn't even get 'em up here to us until after six."

"How come you didn't tell that lady I was taking over the route?"

"Why tell her, she don't care," Summers answered with contempt. "Half the time she don't even answer and the other half she gives you fifty cents. Don't worry,

The Paper Boy's Last Day

I'll introduce you to all the *good* customers."

All at once, with abrupt silence, the streetlights came on along the length of the street. Together the two boys worked along the sidewalk, mounting nearly every porch, pressing the bell or knocking, meeting somebody from within, coming down again. Wind blew from the driveways and caught them between houses. The sky grew dark blue, the houses became black solid projections upward of the dark earth, though lighted from within with various intensities of yellow light. People held their storm doors open against the wind, to pay; the punch snapped on the cold air; the money purse began to weigh upon the tall boy's shoulder; and as they worked up the opposite sidewalk and finally out to Broadway, a main street, the hooded boy's two bags began to hang limp and deflated and they snapped, as he walked, against his knees.

Now they climbed a set of concrete steps and then some wooden ones, up to the lower porch of a two-family house set back but standing high over the main street. There was a dry cleaner's in the downstairs flat of the house next door, which was built lower, at sidewalk level, and on the other side a bright liquor store.

The old paper boy, Summers, gripped an old-fashioned bell that turned like a key and ground it around, twice. Its works growled on the inside of the door, but long ago it had lost its ring. The two boys waited.

"There's somebody up there," muttered Summers at last, and he hammered on the wood of the door with his fist.

Meanwhile the short boy waited with patience, looking around him cheerfully. When Summers popped open the purse for a moment he could not help looking into it and he said, "So it's a pretty good route?"

"It's all right. I never had a week when I didn't make *some* money. It's all right peddling them. What I hate is the collecting."

"That's the best part."

"Sure, now you say that. Wait till you start coming back and coming back and coming back. You know what I hate, is when you're standing out there and you know they're inside — you can hear their radio on, or see somebody through the window — and they still don't answer, they don't even pay any attention. What can you do? You're out there, and you can't get in. God, what I want is a job where you get your money for sure from a boss every week!"

Summers slammed the money purse shut. Seizing the handle of the door with both hands, he shook it until the wide frosted pane rattled. "Like here," he said. "You know Barbara Cooper? She lives up there, her and her mother. The bell doesn't work, so they can't hear you. And you can't go around to the back, because the people downstairs lock the back porch and they're not our customers."

"Barbara Cooper's got sugar diabetes," said the

The Paper Boy's Last Day 65

hooded boy, who stood dreaming and gazing up Broadway at the cars. "Christ, she's thin. I think she has to take a needle every day."

But Summers leaned out across the porch railing. He twisted his neck, trying to get a view of the windows upstairs. Beyond the thin curtains he was able to recognize a small houseplant on the sill inside, and in the curtains themselves a faint catch of light — not from the front room, but coming for sure from a source deeper within the house.

"That's what I mean," he said savagely. "They just go on living in there, and what do we do? We stand out here, and it gets later and later!"

With sharp knuckles he struck this time the frosted glass of the door pane itself. The house was an old one. Like many such wooden two-families it had a single front door, beyond which was a narrow hall with, to one side, a stairwell leading to the flat above. The downstairs windows were all dark, the people were out, unmistakably. Upstairs there was still no sign. Whatever might be going on up there, the life of the house, it continued — high up, remote from the busy street and the paper boys down below. They were shut out and unregarded. And just for this reason Summers, the old carrier, suddenly made a flat paddle of his hand and delivered three smacks against the glass with all his might. The heavy pane popped backward out of its frame all in one piece; like a sheet of gray ice taken from off water, it slid down off Summers' finger ends and crashed into a thousand ringing bits inside on the hall floor.

Then Summers swore, in a furious clear voice. His words penetrated and echoed in the hollow front hall, flickering now, through the paneless door, with shifting lights from the street. The younger boy stood uncertain a moment. Then he hustled clumsily off the porch, impeded by his bags, for he had heard a door open and someone moving on the porch over their heads.

"What's going on? Who is it down there?"

A thin, nervous-appearing woman bent and peered across the upper railing. All she could see was the figure of the hooded boy, crisscrossed with the straps of his bags, hurrying away.

"Is that you, Billy?" she called.

He stopped and turned. The woman, Mrs. Cooper, was hugging her own bare arms. It was very cold on the porch in the wind without a coat. The boy in the hood said nothing, he would not even lift his head. He looked back at Summers, still hidden on the downstairs porch.

The old paper boy's face fell from its momentary fierceness into resignation. He spoke up without moving.

"It's me, Mrs. Cooper. I just broke your window down here."

"And was that you, shouting just now? I just didn't expect I would ever hear talk like that from Billy Summers."

Even standing below with the noises and lights

of the traffic at his back, the younger boy could see that Mrs. Cooper was somehow hurt. Probably she had always liked Summers. He was sure Summers had always treated her politely. But now Summers kept his head and shoulders well in, underneath the porch, so that she could not see him.

"I'm sorry, Mrs. Cooper," he said from there, quite loud. "I broke your window. I'll have to pay for it."

"Just a minute," the woman called. The hall light came on. She came downstairs, stepping carefully among the pieces of glass at the bottom. Through the opening she looked closely into the face of the old paper boy. "Whatever made you do that?" she asked.

"Nothing — I was just knocking, and it fell out. I'll pay for it."

"But why should you have to knock so hard? This window was here for years and it never fell out. It's as old as the house is."

The old paper boy stared straight at the wallpaper inside. His face was set. Moving up beside him, the hooded boy was struck with how much older than himself Summers was, he remembered all at once that Summers would be through high school this year while he himself was only twelve. Summers was a full head taller, his face sharp and hard. He said only, "I'll clean it up, if you've got a broom or something."

The woman, Mrs. Cooper, too, seemed suddenly quite old. Her eyes watched Summers for a moment, and when they saw he would not look at her, her mouth set.

"Yes — I think you'd better."

She went back upstairs. The next thing, the two boys watched her hands set out on the landing a broom, a dustpan and a wastebasket. With his eyes fixed on the upstairs door, now firmly closed, Summers went up.

It took him a very short time to clean up the glass. He placed Mrs. Cooper's things neatly at the bottom of the stairs and the two boys went down to the sidewalk together. They started walking.

"Why did you do that, Summers?" the younger boy asked. He was really troubled. "Now you'll have to pay for that window. You'll hardly make anything this week."

"I don't know — it's my last day, I guess is all. She's a nice woman, but I always hated collecting them. They'd sit there and sit there. This wasn't just the first time. And act like they never even heard you."

"Maybe she really couldn't hear. Maybe she's hard of hearing. There's the front door and all the way upstairs, and all this noise in the street."

"No," said the older boy, his eyebrows concentrated. "It don't make any difference, whether they could hear me or not. I was a pretty good paper boy. I didn't miss anybody much. I never missed them. I always came pretty early. Every Friday night I was out there, and they wouldn't come down. I couldn't make them take notice. I used to wonder what they were *doing* up there in that house, and me outside. Damn it, you see how she came down tonight? They came to the door!"

The Paper Boy's Last Day

The tall boy stretched his longer legs excitedly. Bags flapping, the younger one struggled to keep up.

"Aren't we missing houses?" he called. "We got this one, haven't we?"

Summers halted. He brought out a cigarette from one pocket and a cigarette lighter from another, and strolled back. "Yeah — throw one up," he answered. "Just throw up the paper for all the rest of 'em. We got enough money to pay the bill by now. We can get the rest of these houses tomorrow morning. I'll come to your house."

The Ambulance Driver

The Ambulance Driver

A circle of people had gathered one night on the sidewalk around a parked ambulance. The red light on top was flashing and the motor running, as though there were not a moment to be lost in bearing some stricken human being to a place where his life would be safe. The circle of people extended up to the door of a house that most of them knew very well but had never been inside of, which was now thrown open and a part of its mysterious interior — the hallway at least — revealed for the first time. They saw a man come hustling out on one end of a stretcher — though it was not really a stretcher; it had chromium-plated handles at each end and some sort of carriage with wheels underneath so that it could stand by itself if necessary, or be rolled — the long covered body following through the doorway, with only the face exposed, and then the second ambulance man coming, awkward and careful not to stumble, showing effort in his expression. His name was Baer.

The Ambulance Driver

He was a large, quite heavy man, whose wide black belt with the big metal buckle gave him a look of physical solidity, wearing a uniform that included dark trousers with a bright stripe running down on both sides: a man performing in the presence of crowds of people with a perfect intentness on his business, perfectly at home in the atmosphere of life-or-death excitement that had gathered the crowd in the first place, acting as though it were his sphere — as indeed it was.

The ambulance men hurried their burden to the ambulance, set it down an instant, flung wide the rear door, which hung open high, at an angle; the stretcher was rolled in on its carriage; the intern — all in white, very young-looking — came hurrying out through the open house door, which he left open. He climbed into the back of the vehicle with the patient. Baer secured them inside together and hastened forward to the steering wheel; his partner was already waiting on the other side. The ambulance jumped into motion, and now the very blinking of its red light seemed to speed up, becoming more urgent; other vehicles fell away to the side in its path as it screamed toward the hospital.

In a scene like this, though he was never guilty of an expression or gesture either vain or unnecessary, Baer was certainly conscious of his own important part. Yet after all, driving an ambulance is a job like any other and he had come by it in the way that people generally find jobs.

He had hardly begun his working life when the

depression came on the country. For awhile it was all anybody talked about — though, apparently, the real depression had begun three or four years earlier in New York City with a number of men leaping to their deaths from the windows of high buildings. For Baer, who was willing to do anything at all, it was not so hard to find a job in those times as to keep one. Every job he found would end after a few months.

Then one day he went to the hospital. A friend had told him that they kept guinea pigs there in coops, for the doctors to experiment with, and rabbits and white mice, and that they might need a man to feed the animals and clean out the coops.

Baer asked about the guinea pigs. The fierce gray-haired woman in the white uniform, whom he was sent in to see, looked at him hard and asked instead: "Can you drive?" Baer didn't flinch. He had used a truck for two days on a farm, once; he said yes. "Would you work nights?" Baer said he would. "Would you work twelve hours, every night?" Baer said he would. "Well, it isn't any of my business and I don't know why they sent you to me," said the woman, "but I know the hospital needs a night ambulance driver." She sent him to the right person to see, and he was hired.

He worked from seven in the evening until seven in the morning. At certain times of the year, that would be almost exactly from darkness until light, a term of work that seemed normal to Baer; he did not feel himself abused by the long hours. And then the work was not really hard. He and his partner, a man named Freddy, who was a little older than himself, sat in wooden chairs out in front of the garage attached to the big partially lighted hospital and looked something like firemen waiting for a call. Freddy had been handling things alone, and was glad enough to help Baer with his driving. It turned out that one night a week Baer did have to look after the guinea pigs, but he didn't mind that. He was used to animals; his parents had always kept chickens and even, for a time, rabbits. They lived almost in the country, just beyond the last paved street. Baer got one night off each week, but it could not be on a weekend.

When the hospital job had lasted for a year and seemed secure ("People will always get sick," his father said to him wisely), Baer got married on the strength of it. He had been going with the same girl for more than four years, but he was a careful man, strictly brought up to believe he must always be responsible for his own, and he had put off marrying. Even when the jobs had not lasted he had saved his money. Now he moved with his wife — a black-haired girl, slim, but wiry and strong, whose family had lived at the city's edge near his own for years — into a flat in a two-family house just a few blocks from the hospital.

For the next few years their life was successful enough. But then Baer said to his wife, "I don't like living in somebody else's house." And his wife said, "You say what you want us to do. As long as the roof don't leak and the floors don't sag, I don't care."

So Baer looked around, and in the sandy country to the north of the city he found a little place that had been empty for awhile: exactly square, with decent siding though the paint was bad, and a four-sided pyramid for a roof. The roof was covered with tar strips, the kind that are sprinkled on one side with abrasive particles like sugar, which glint in the sun. It was tiny but cheap; it sat well back on a narrow piece of land bounded on one side by a line of medium-sized oak trees, and was on a paved road about seven miles from the hospital. Freddy found a used Model A Ford for Baer to buy, and they moved out.

Immediately Baer and his wife went to work. They made the place a human habitation. (Between themselves, they sometimes wondered what it could have been before.) They had a well dug; its pipe came up to feed a neat little hand pump mounted at the side of the kitchen sink. They bought a small oil heater for warmth in the main room, but slept under quilts in a cold bedroom. The place was already wired. In the first days (they had moved out in summer) Baer's wife scrubbed and disinfected the inside and began to make it pleasant. Just because she had lived in the country, where dirt is plentiful, she would not bear it, and everything must be shining-sanitary. The place would smell of furniture polish, kerosene, disinfectant, sometimes of an oversweet smoking incense stick, but never of mustiness or dirt. Yet there were also the small touches of decoration — the house plants, crocheted doilies on chair arms, miniature articles arranged on corner shelves — that attach people to the peculiar sheltering interior, even a single room, that they inhabit. In the meantime Baer sacrificed some of his sleeping hours. He added a shedlike wing at the back. He dug a deep hole and over it erected an outhouse around which he built a lattice, and at the base of the lattice he planted morning glory vines. As he had no real skill his work was crude but strong, like a peasant's. He never hesitated to build what he needed though he could manage only the simplest tools — saw and hammer and nails. He did everything directly, in the simplest way.

  Every night at the same time Baer came out of the little house, got into his Model A, drove out the long driveway, which turned twice around some small pines, and rolled off toward the city. Each morning about seven-thirty he was back. Winter or summer, the open days passed over the house with a profound and quiet peacefulness. Inside, Baer slept. Sometimes his wife came out, slight and strong, bearing a great basket, and hung out glistening clothes on a rope that stretched to the oak trees. In summer the scent of sweet fern was hot and strong in the sun, and the hot tar of the roof had its own smell; but in all seasons the air carried the tang of the lime that Baer's wife used in the outhouse. The land itself was pleasant. There were many small birches on the place. The whippoorwills were very loud in the first part of the night, after Baer had left, but they didn't bother Mrs. Baer; she liked them.

Nothing much seemed to happen. One year Baer's wife had a baby, a girl, but even this event did not disturb their life at all. Baer simply took his wife in with him when he went to work one night and brought her back again holding a pink blanket-bundle in her arms when he returned at his usual time in the morning about ten days later. From then on a carriage would be seen outside sometimes, draped with gauze netting to keep away insects. The baby was happy, it never cried, and so kept intact the perfect sunfilled serenity that hung over Baer's house and land.

Such, at least, was the picture of Baer's life held by Henry Renfrew, the young engineer who had bought land on the other side of the oak trees and built a house for himself and his wife. For the Second World War had come and gone without affecting Baer at all. He was not quite too old for the service, but at the very end of the age group, and besides, they told him there was something the matter with him — his teeth were going rotten. He might have made a lot of money at the G.E. Works, but he was too canny; the war wouldn't last forever, he figured, but people would always get sick. After the war, in the general rush to the suburbs, the sandy plots with their cover of birches, pine, oak and sweet fern began to be bought up along his road. Renfrew came, and built his new white wooden house of the Cape Cod type. It stood just beyond the long straight oak branches, close to the property line.

Henry Renfrew was doing well at the G.E. He

was smart, and liked to read. He had not been in the war either. He liked the idea of living in the country. And from the first, he took an interest in his neighbor — this large uniformed man who, in the morning, was just driving in when he was driving out; who came out and left for work just as he himself was eating his supper and looking forward to the hours of enjoyment ahead. The sunny peacefulness of Baer's property that he would observe on weekends (the Baers went to church and returned and disappeared into their house and all was as before) appealed to his imagination, and so did the idea of a man who spent his days sleeping in a place like this and then went down into the city where throughout the night he raced among the darkened houses with a siren, penetrating always into some of them with the extraordinary right possessed by those who act in emergencies. When Renfrew took a free moment at the Works, and read about some awful accident in the city the night before, it would suddenly occur to the young man that of course Baer had been there.

In these years Baer's little girl had been growing. Already she was four and a half years old. Another year, and she would go to kindergarten. Baer and his wife were proud of her. If they spoke of her to anyone it was "our daughter" this and "our daughter" that. Of course they spoiled her terribly, though they considered, themselves, that they were too severe. Baer kept a strap on a nail behind the kitchen door and he wasn't slow about using it, so that the child screamed, in rebel-

The Ambulance Driver

lion as well as in pain, until at times she lost her breath and was reduced to gasps which only came with the sucking-in of her breath, involuntarily. He didn't beat her in anger but only when he and his wife decided it was necessary. At bottom he was a sentimental man. He would actually cry, at sorrowful things; his eyes would grow red and real tears would come. He loved the little girl and so did his wife, and he did many unexpected little things for her out of the simple impulses of his love.

About this time the regular guinea-pig keeper brought in a puppy for one of the daytime drivers — whose wife, that night, swore she would leave him if he tried to bring it into the house. So the man drove back with the dog to the hospital where Baer, thinking suddenly of his little girl, took it from him.

Next morning he brought it home. The creature was so young and fat that its belly dragged between its weak legs in the sand of the driveway. The little girl was overjoyed. She had never had playmates; she was too old for the smaller children that people like the Renfrews were just beginning to have. She named the dog George. Eventually it grew into a mongrel with the lean body and legs of a terrier but the ears and face and curved tail of a small hound. Then in the green and black scrub of Baer's land the bright clothing of the girl would flash out, winding through the cover, together with the swift white body of the dog.

The autumn came again. Baer's daughter went out in the morning now to catch the yellow school bus on the paved road. Baer slept. His wife did her work. The land lay under bright sunlight. The dog George played with a black shadow in and among the small, nervous, shining heart-shaped birch leaves in a grove at the woods line behind the house.

One afternoon in November the girl did not see George when she got off the bus. She changed her clothes and ran out to the birch grove. Soon she was running back again, zigzagging through the brush, yelling madly. George lay in an open shallow hole in the loose sand, suckling twelve piglike, pink-tinged puppies. It seemed important enough to wake Baer, whose sleep was never intruded upon, and he too was led out to the edge of the land. And while the girl squatted and gingerly touched the warm bodies, Baer's wife looked at him across the shallow burrow. With the years it seemed she had grown only more lean and strong and her eyes, once brown, appeared now positively black, glowing and alive and black.

"It's this sand that keeps 'em warm," Baer muttered uncomfortably. "Sun shines on it all day long." The two went back to the house.

Inside, Baer's wife said, "We can't feed twelve dogs, Cap."

Baer scratched his head. His mouth tasted terrible; he had been waked up two hours before his time.

"You know yourself we've only got so much a

week," she said. "You aren't ever going to make much more. We've got this place, but we've always had to watch. Everything they eat up will come out of our mouths." Baer scratched his head. His wife picked up a dust cloth and used it a little, without thinking. "It's hard enough to give away one or two," she went on. "Where are we going to give away a dozen?" Instead of answering, Baer went back to the bedroom to sleep.

Purposely Baer left the litter out in the half-exposed lair. But though the nights were cold, the dogs throve; they grew into fat little pigs such as George had been when Baer first brought her home. They squealed a great deal, especially when the mother left them to be fed herself, and when she returned and settled down among them. In two weeks they had begun to wobble in and out of the sweet fern.

"They'll never die now," Baer's wife said to him.

Accordingly, on a cold Saturday afternoon Baer got out of bed a couple of hours early. He dressed in his hospital uniform. In the shed he found a big cardboard grocery box with flaps he could fold together at the top, which he carried outdoors to the back of the Model A. He took out his knife and squatted in the shelter of the automobile. The day was windy, with fast-moving low clouds.

"What are you doing, Cap?" the girl asked him, coming to the house from the dogs. (It was a peculiarity of the household that Baer's daughter, as well as his wife, called him Cap.)

"Don't talk to me now," he said.

She watched him cut a hole in the box quite near to the top, perhaps an inch and a half across. Then he took the box by one flap and walked with it out through the dry sweet fern. The little girl trailed. The puppies began to bleat as he pulled them off the mother and dropped them into the box. Now he needed both hands; he had to grasp the box by the bottom edges as he walked back with the wiggling and scratching animals inside. The live load, from which came a solitary yelp or two, but strangely none of the frantic squealing of the last weeks, caused the tall box to pitch in his hands.

"What are you going to do?" cried the girl, running after him.

"I'm going to put them to sleep," Baer said in a loud voice. But he did not look at her; his face was intent, instead, on what he was doing.

From the side the child, running and stumbling among the fern bushes, hardly able to keep up, looked at him suspiciously.

"Will it hurt them?"

"It will put them to sleep," he repeated obstinately, with even greater seriousness about his task.

He had reached the back end of the Ford, which stood quite high on its narrow wheels. Stooping down, setting the box on the ground, he fitted the projecting exhaust pipe into the hole he had made with his knife.

Then he went round, climbed into the car, and turned over the engine. The four cylinders began to work in regular, tinny, fluttering cycles. Baer set the hand throttle and walked back to the rear of the car.

Something — a light body wound in soft clothes — flew at him out of somewhere and hit him a tremendous shock, so that he staggered. Baer's little girl had fastened on and was biting his big arm in its uniform jacket, her small feet kicking at the stripes on his trouser legs. Without thinking, Baer righted himself and flung out his arm; the body flew and landed and lay limp among its clothes. But in an instant it was up, and at him again as though by electric attraction. This time Baer set his face toward the box, which was vibrating ever so slightly with the regular flutter of the car's engine. Inside were scratchings and now the sharp mother-squeals of the last two weeks. He caught the girl more gently, but with the back of his iron arm, and flung her ten feet away, though he never looked at her. She did not lose her feet. She came on again, and he warded her off.

The child began to scream in a voice so high that it could not be loud, running back and forth in an arc a little distance from him. Baer would get angry sometimes and when he did he used rough words that the girl had heard, and now she used them against him, screeching them out until, as when he beat her, she had to stop and gasp for breath. From one side the noise brought Baer's wife outdoors; and from the other, up to the line of oak trees that limited his property, it brought Henry Renfrew.

The chugging Model A, the cardboard box from which the squeals came, the hysterical little girl, Baer's intent face — the young man took the whole thing in immediately.

"For God's sake, Baer!" he cried out in appeal.

The ambulance driver's expression shattered at once, like a flowerpot. "You want to take them?" he yelled, turning savagely on the younger man. "You're rich — you got a new house." And the big uniformed man suddenly advanced upon his neighbor, his eyes red, his hair disheveled with sweat under his policeman's cap. "Here," he shouted in a fury, "you say you'll take them, and I'll shut off the engine! Well? You going to take them?"

The engineer turned and went back to his house. His aluminum storm door banged shut.

Baer watched him all the way. Slowly he returned to the Model A, which had never ceased to flutter — and flutter — and flutter.

Baer's wife had managed to get their daughter into the house. Baer himself stood with folded arms over the box, and waited. He stood an unbearably long time; he even thought of the gasoline the car must be consuming during such a long time. After a while Baer's wife and the girl came out of the house and stood by the back door. They were both quiet.

But when finally he turned off the engine and pulled open the box's flaps the little girl was there, peer-

The Ambulance Driver

ing in, as soon as he was. And three of the little animals were still squirming and pushing forward, their noses buried against the soft bodies of the others. She reached far in and grabbed them and ran into the house with them before Baer could think.

He shook his head. He dragged the others out to the back of his land and buried them deep in the sandy ground. Then he threw the box into his trash pit and set fire to it. He looked at his wristwatch. It was getting late.

He entered the kitchen, first wiping his feet outside, and sat down and waited to be served his supper. While he ate, his wife told him that the child had the puppies in the bedroom — the farthest corner of the square house from Baer himself at that moment.

Afterward Baer went out to the shed off the kitchen and rummaged in his wife's rag bag until he found a shirt that no longer fit him — he was growing more stout, thicker in the chest and arms. He came in and sat down again at the table.

In the bedroom his wife said to the little girl, "He won't hurt them now. He has to go to work. You can get them some milk. I'll stay here with them."

As she came through the kitchen the child took the way that would keep her farthest from Baer, eyeing him with terror the whole time. They kept their icebox outside in the unheated shed. As soon as he heard the handles snapping out there Baer got up and hurried quietly into the bedroom. His wife had the puppies. He spread the shirt, and she placed them in it. He gathered the edges around them, and made a great knot; he knotted both sleeves. Little squeals came from the bundle. He thrust it underneath his jacket and walked straight out of the house. The girl was working with a milk bottle and a pie tin at the kitchen table as he passed through.

Baer drove toward the city faster than he had ever driven his car before, but without the firm control he always had over the speeding ambulance. Outside, it had turned very cold. The wind attacked the high square car in irregular fits, as though something were trying to snatch it up and shake it. Although he was early, it was already nearly dark. Instead of going to the hospital Baer drove to a highway near the river. He stopped the car, picked up the knotted shirt from the floor in back, and got out.

Immediately the pups began their squealing. All around the whole earth was dark, but the broad sky was light enough, with deep gray-black smoking clouds driving through it, throwing down sharp bits of rain. He started to walk through a wide field, all stubble now, nothing in it but himself, toward the river at its far verge. Carrying the shirt — he couldn't help himself — he looked upward, back and over his shoulder, and he only wished he could be under trees, or in a building somewhere. He was a religious man. From boyhood he had felt, at certain times, the presence of someone watching everything he did. He had wondered, sometimes,

The Ambulance Driver

about the men who had had to kill during the war. Still, he set his face and walked on across the stubble. He was responsible. Men living in the world are responsible for themselves and theirs.

He came to the river bank — curving here, the field shelving off a little each year — and slid down the bank right into the water; he felt the cold water suddenly encircle his ankles. He leaned out deeper, and with both hands sank the light-colored shirt. The bodies struggled under his hands; he could actually hear the whimpers, though they were submerged. Harder he pressed down — holding them down. His shoes were sunk in river mud. Both his arms, and his two feet, grew numb. The forms had long been still. Baer lifted out the dripping bundle, scrambled up the bank and carried it toward the car. Vaguely in his mind was the idea that he would take them back and bury them "right" on his land.

But when he pushed back the driver's seat and dropped the wet shirt on the back floor, two distinct, despairing squeals sounded from inside it.

The big man caught up the shirt like a maniac and lumbered across the stubble field wildly and recklessly, falling twice. When at last he came to the top of the bank, he leaned back and hurled the wet bundle high and far from him, out over the dark river.

He stood panting, all muddy, listening. Incredibly, he heard nothing. For one instant hallucinations overcame him — something had caught it out there, where he could not see, and was bearing it up to the last light places in the sky. But he had only forgotten what a strong man he was, and at last, far out upon the water, he heard the single sound — splash.

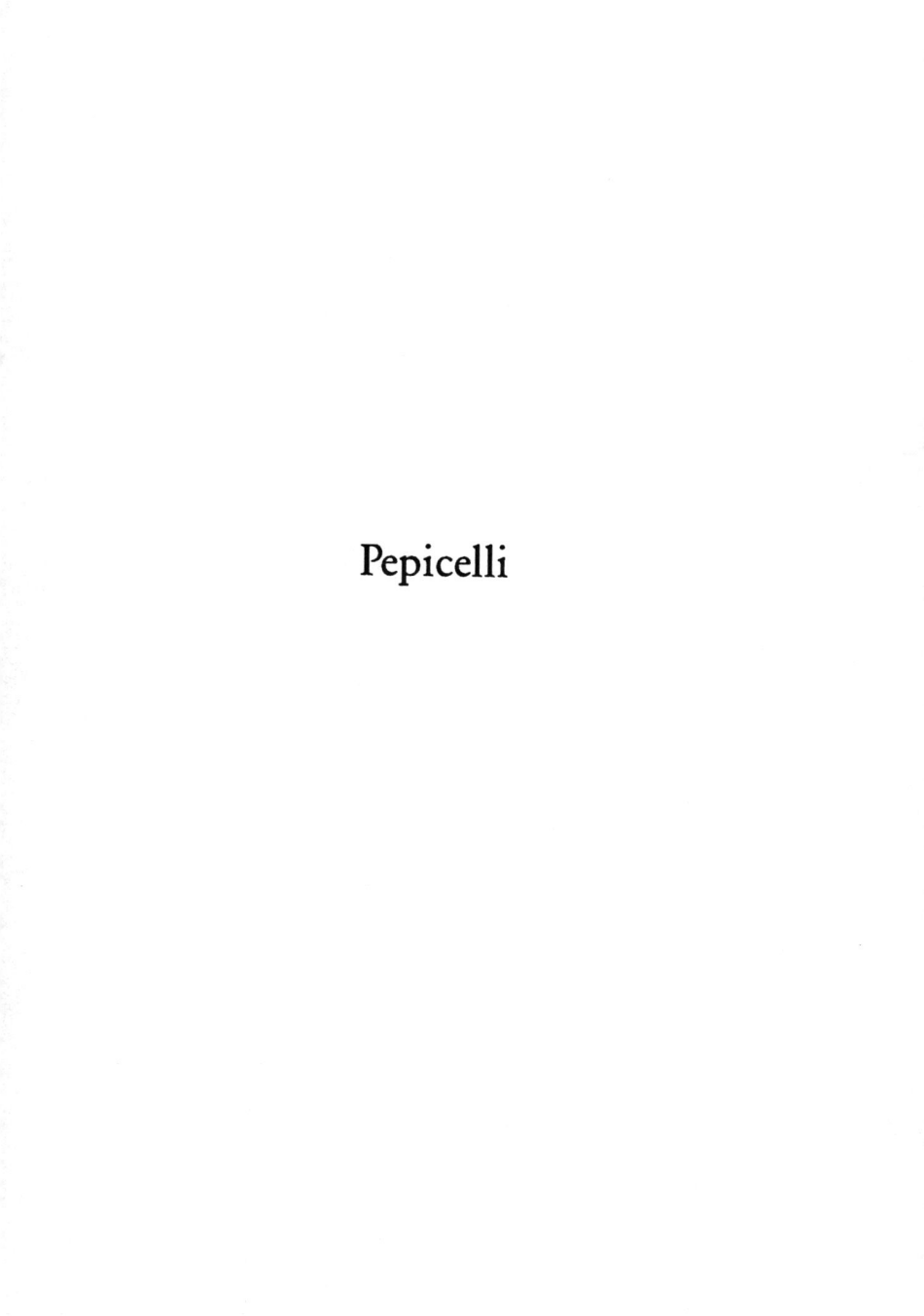

Pepicelli

Pepicelli

Pepicelli: he came half-running home one night around seven-thirty, pushing the thing in front of him. It was a motorcycle of all things, which was pretty much what Kate said to herself when she saw it coming up the street from the front window of the flat. It was something to look at anyway, you really didn't see that many motorcycles on Third Street, and then it was mostly young kids in big leather belts, and hats like state troopers, or something; big shots, a lot littler than the thing they were riding though, just sitting up there on their behinds until it ran away on them one day and killed them. You didn't see the squirts like that pushing the things either, they might get their big gloves or something else dirty. But here came somebody pushing this one, hopping along, puffing, in the almost-dark; a little man, but thick enough, who might be anywhere from thirty-eight or thirty-nine to fifty years old. He was as a matter of fact forty-six. His name was Pepicelli and he was Kate's husband — something she didn't really want to believe until the motorcycle turned, like a big black dog, took a bite of the curb, then jumped it and went trotting out the alleyway that led to the Pepicellis', and the people living upstairs', backyard. Pretty soon you could call it just the Pepicellis' backyard as Pepicelli was meaning to buy the house. Seeing they were there going on twenty-five years, it was about time.

Motorcycle or not Kate had been waiting for him, and now he had shown up she went out to warm supper. It wasn't any wonder he was late — he was probably afraid somebody might see him pushing a thing like that up the street in daylight.

Just at dark Nick, the man next door, liked to hose down his grass. He saw the big cycle come rolling out from the alley, and Pepicelli running with it but sort of hanging on behind, like a boy exercising a big black horse. Pepicelli, moving, shuffling, breathing heavily, trotted it in an arc across his grass, around and into an open space between his house siding and Nick's fence. There it stood up by itself. Pepicelli had never had a garage.

He let go the grips and came out between the machine and the fence, and there was Nick, come up on his side.

"Holy smoke," said Nick. "What kind of thing do you call that?" Although like Kate he saw very well what it was. Pepicelli, still breathing hard, told him as much.

"What do you care, Nick? You see it."

Pepicelli

Nick edged down along the fence to see it better. The thing was big, long, black, the handlebars wide black antlers, wheels as big as a car's, silver-rimmed, the saddle a size for two men.

That was a good-sized machine, Nick said; and he asked what it was for. But Pepicelli, back a little from the fence, squatting, was running his hot fingers through the grass. It was a heavy thing. It had put a track in his lawn. When he rose he could feel his legs. Nick was agreeing, the sons of bitches weighed, and what was she, a Harley-Davidson? — They used to make the best ones when he was a kid. When Pepicelli was a kid. "You should of rode her home," said Nick.

"Let me see that hose," said Pepicelli. "I need a drink."

Nick watched this little Pepicelli, who looked so hot and jumpy and worked up, while he drank. "You're as old as I am," said Nick. "Hell." And he asked again, if Pepicelli had said she was a Harley-Davidson.

"I don't know," said Pepicelli. "I just bought it. Off a kid. Don't ask me so much unless you want to buy it."

Nick said, sure, he could just see himself. But he wasn't the one who had bought her, Pepicelli was.

Pepicelli stood for a moment in the dark. The sweat was beginning to cool on him, he had drunk some water, and now he could give some attention to this idea, of him having the motorcycle. He thought it was like having his own house, the same kind of thing, he would have to take care of her. He didn't have a garage, though his brother-in-law did; but just a canvas to throw over her would be better, it would keep her home, where he could keep his eye on her. She was a big machine, and worth something, and had to be taken care of. That was what he thought about it just then.

Nick had a tarp; Pepicelli said he wanted it. Nick said, to wait a minute, he'd shut off his hose and find it; and he went around the bulk of his house. He came back with a piece of stiff parafinned canvas that he and Pepicelli, on either side of the fence, tucked around the big motorcycle. Nick had to say again, by God, that was some machine; and he wanted to know, how long Pepicelli would want his tarp.

Pepicelli was strung-up, he felt reckless, he said things. Maybe he'd buy his own tarp and when he did, Nick would get his back. Or tell Nick what, he'd hang onto this one, and Nick could take it out in rides. Him and Nick, they'd ride to work every day; save Nick's gas. Nick wasn't worrying about his gas, Pepicelli paid him for it anyway. "That's what you think you bought her for, is it?" he asked.

Pepicelli said, sure, Nick, and thought to himself, what did it matter what you said to Nick. Nick on his side was thinking, Pepicelli, he'd kill himself, he'd wrap around a pole, he'd break his neck, he was crazy. Pepicelli and him, they'd ride to work — sure, Nick!

❖

Kate was waiting in the kitchen, where things were warm again and ready, as they had been at a quarter to six and nobody had shown up to eat them. She had made up her mind she was going to make a little noise about it, but Pepicelli never gave her much trouble like that. She could think of times, years ago, when they wouldn't see her father for days. But that was years ago, and now even he didn't do it anymore, if only because he hadn't any place to go, no place not to come back from, Kate thought.

Kate's maiden name was Brennan. This father of hers had worked all his life for the Department of Parks and Recreation. His wife was dead some years now; he himself still lived with an unmarried son in the house where, when he wasn't working or nobody knew where he was, he had brought up six other sons and his wife had brought up Kate. When Kate was something over eighteen her father had brought home a young man named Pepicelli, twenty-two, who also worked for the City, and who was, her father said, "a steady boy." Kate's mother might have been doubtful at first, but she came around to Pepicelli before the year was out. Old Brennan spent most of the wedding reception telling his wife, one way and another, how pleased he was, as Kate was his only daughter and for that reason the last woman he'd have to worry about taking care of.

Right after the wedding the two of them, Kate and Pepicelli, had moved into the house on Third Street. They had lived in the upstairs flat for the first five years, and all that time there was plenty to do. The house was not so old then, but it was not in such good shape either. It needed everything done to it, inside and outside too: painting and papering, roofing, repointing the chimney; new plumbing; the foundation rebuilt in back; walks and driveway repoured, and then the yard cleared and graded and seeded and fenced-off, finally, with a space for a garden. They had worked very hard because after all, as Pepicelli would say, they were the ones going to live in the place; but partly, too, because the landlord, who lived downstairs then, kept the rent low and talked about selling to Pepicelli. He never did, but after he moved out Pepicelli became something like the man of the house, collecting the rent from the new people down below. By that time they were well settled in Third Street.

They liked it there. Pepicelli worked in the parks with old Brennan, who had got him the job. But Kate and Pepicelli found themselves having less and less to do with the older couple, what with the all the work on the house, and after five years they never even went to the old place, except that Kate might go, to see her mother; but later on the older woman would have to come to Third Street when she wanted to see them. The father never came with her, but once he showed up by himself. Pepicelli said, well! to come into the house, and did he want to drink something? He did; and they drank together. Then they got up, and Pepicelli leading, away they went: all over the house, out front, around back — the older man had to see it all. He had a fine time, too, just couldn't keep from laughing, and every time Pepicelli stopped, and pointed, and started talking, Brennan took him under his arm and looked at him sideways and grinned, and leaned upon him so hard that Pepicelli could hardly keep his feet. Around they went. Brennan laughed, listened, leaned on his shoulder, thought it was all "pretty good"; Pepicelli said, he guessed it was. The older man left, and come back, said Pepicelli, come see us again; but he never did, and Kate and Pepicelli didn't expect him to, just as they'd never expected him the first time. Pepicelli still saw him at work, until he got a better job that was more permanent than just a laborer, a little city park to take care of alone, with a tool shed on it. After that the mother died, there was a funeral, and then there was nothing at all between the old house and Third Street. Once in a while they saw one of the married brothers, the one who had the garage Pepicelli was thinking of.

  Pepicelli and his wife got older. They didn't think much about it. The only thing that seemed to change was the rent, which after long years went suddenly higher. Pepicelli still collected from the people downstairs, but he had lost contact with the owner and dealt with a downtown real estate agent. Just lately he learned that the owner had died, in New York City somewhere, and he started to deal with the agent about buying the house. And this night, when he hadn't come home, that was where Kate had expected he would be. But here he came, now, with something she didn't even want to think about — that great big machine.

She heard him outside mounting the back steps. She hurried over and pulled open the door. In walked Pepicelli, right past her where she stood. He saw her, well enough; was there any reason for expecting not to see her? She watched him. He went straight to the sink, turned on the faucet, passed his hands and wrists under the water. He slapped his face, his neck, his entire head, with the water. His shirt was all wet; he made noises, he snorted. Kate watched him. He snapped down a dishtowel and scrubbed himself with it. She didn't like it at all, a person should do all that in the bathroom.

Pepicelli turned around, but now it was she who was busy; you know, she could be preoccupied too, with the stove and the putting things on the table. Sit down, she told him. He did. She told him shortly to go ahead, start, don't wait for her; and after a little she sat down herself, and watched him.

Pretty nice, she started in, the way some people could run around all night and still have supper waiting for them, the minute they got home! Didn't worry about anything, just took care of their little selves; didn't try to call people up; as if nobody had a telephone any more!

Pepicelli on his side went right on eating. He felt better from the water, but he was still all tightened up, light-headed, tired in his legs. He was thinking about that motorcycle, and about Nick, that nosy Nick, who had everything so figured-out all the time. All this was running around in his head, but all of a sudden it stopped. Pepicelli listened. He heard his wife talking; talking at him. What about it, she wanted to know, did he find out about the house, or not? Pepicelli answered, no, he didn't have time to go downtown.

O no, Kate said, she saw what kind of things he had time for, kid's tricks. What did he think he was doing, bringing one of those things around here? Did he think he was one of those squirt kids? — One of those squirt kids! repeated Kate, who except for her mother was the biggest person in both houses she'd lived in.

It was true Pepicelli was a small man; but he was thick-set, sturdy, with a kind of density that made him slow to be moved. Now he told his wife to close up her mouth; this was a man's business. At the same time he looked at her at last, quietly, but so serious that Kate was flustered, she wouldn't say frightened. But she rose up and moved to the stove, where from behind her turned back she muttered, business, some business; nice business.

To which Pepicelli paid no attention, but finished eating in a very deliberate way.

Afterward he went into the living room, where in one corner they kept a tall cabinet with shelves for books and knickknacks on top, and lower down a door that could be pulled down and used as a desk to write at, with little drawers and cubbyholes in which were bills, bank-books, receipts, rent books, tax forms, pens, ink, blotters, paper clips, stamps — all the officialdom having to do with the Pepicellis, including marriage license and birth certificates. Pepicelli unlocked this door, lowered it, brought over a chair, sat down to it. He wrote out a check for a hundred dollars, payable to the kid, blotted it, filled in the stub, blotted that; entered the payment in a separate notebook, slipped the check into an envelope that he sealed, stamped, addressed to the kid's mother, and blotted. He dried his pen, put things away, closed up and set the envelope out an upper shelf, to go. Then he sat down heavily in an armchair because, he told himself, he was tired.

He supposed he had a right to be tired. He had been up early. After breakfast he had strolled in the early light up and down on his sidewalk until Nick, tired and without much to say, backed the car into the street. Nick had dropped him at his park. There he walked in his steady way across the grass, while the squirrels ran around like crazy things, jabbering, chasing one another up and down trees, and he said to himself they were funny little buggers. Once at the little brick tool house he thought he would wait a bit for the kid to show up but then he remembered, this was the day, the kid wasn't going to show at all. So he had set bushel baskets and a rake in the wheelbarrow, walked the barrow out in front of him, and started to rake up the grass he had cut the day before behind a power mower.

For a while he worked. The squirrels had tired themselves out; it was very quiet. The sun rose higher, the loose grass dried in it. He pulled off his jacket and hung it on one handle of the wheelbarrow. No cars passed along the street beside the park. Nobody showed themselves over there. Then, about nine o'clock, had come from off behind the houses, sound; muttering, humming, roaring and thundering; metallic, and more; staccato, yet undulating even in this; bursts of expression shortly and sharply strung together in a kind of announcement making itself heard from somewhere beyond the row of houses. Pepicelli, at his raking, listened; he thought it must be a motorcycle, or something very like it, and he wondered, whether it might be the kid. Then in a sudden moment he had found out: the sound had swollen, sharpened, and there had come running up the street the cycle — big, black, the kid up on her, easy and jaunty and then quickly crouched up forward as she roared in a burst of the engine, took the driveway, came down running on the cinderpath and wheeled, not breaking stride at all, to tear across the grass at Pepicelli with a rush that was more than just the sound, the kid now sitting back and high on the big machine, knee-gripping her, calling in a high kid's voice that came with the rush at Pepicelli, who stepped back grasping his rake as the kid tore by between his grass-filled baskets: "Pep...i...cellleeeee!": which was part of the rush of the thing and went off streaming after it, over the cinderpath, across the ball diamond, up into the wooded hills behind, where Pepicelli could hear it, and see it now and then plunging, wheeling, shaking the brush, rattling the leaves of living trees. And then the kid had brought her back, raging down from the hills like some raiding barbarian, across the diamond and the grass and again to Pepicelli, still clutching his rake; where the kid stopped her, pulled her back, but kept one knee dug into her, while she roared and roared under the hand throttle and dug and pawed at the ground as he played with the clutch, bouncing a little, cocky, in the saddle, a thin young kid who grinned and yelled with the roar and snort of the machine: "Pepicellee! Buy her? — Hunnerd dollars!" Off again, in a spurt of torn-out grass and dirt to the edge of the open, skidding, wheeling, pivoting around the kid's grounded leg, then up, straightaway at Pepicelli who stood there, grinned a little and thought, what a bastard kid, but watched closely, more and more so as the big machine lunged, pawed, raced past him in another — "Hunnerd dollars!" — rush, to be kicked around again by the kid for another pass — "Hunnerd dollars!" — and so again until, the next time, Pepicelli had grinned and nodded and when the kid had called out the — "Hunnerd dollars!" — he had said it with him; so after the next pivot the kid had throttled her to a rolling trot and then a walk across the grass and she had come rolling, bouncing slightly on her shocks, to where Pepicelli stood with his rake.

So they had made the agreement, Pepicelli still grinning. The kid tried to teach him about the cycle.

Look here, old Pepicelli, see this thing? Watch now; and Pepicelli looked and the kid said, you watching, old Pepicelli? Shut up, he was, said Pepicelli, and then something would happen with the machine. Finally the kid drove it out behind the tool shed and came walking back. He was going into the army, he had to be there by noon.

At the end of the work day Pepicelli had pushed his wheelbarrow slowly back to the tool house and locked up. Then he had wheeled the big motorcycle out to the street. He had rolled her home, all the way to the other side of the city. It had taken him three hours.

And now he was very tired. He judged it would be a good thing to go to bed early, right away would be very good. He pulled himself from his chair and standing, felt himself very very heavy and tired, too tired to be able to think, even.

Next morning when Pepicelli awoke his wife was already out of bed. Out the window he could see close up the gray boards of Nick's house. He crossed from the bed to a chair by the window, which sat there dressed in his clothes. One by one he pulled them off, and onto himself; and when the chair was bare he sat down on it to pull on and lace up his work shoes. The sun was on the topmost bricks of Nick's chimney. Pepicelli stood up and raised the window all the way, to air out the room.

When he entered the kitchen there was Kate

standing at the stove, her back turned, almost as if she had stood there all night long, as if in fact she stood there perpetually, through all their life together; for Pepicelli was really most used to seeing her just like that. Whenever he was at work and he thought of his wife for a moment, that was what he would see — the full back of a large woman wearing a clean cotton dress, her thick, dry dark hair braided and rolled up neatly at the back of her head; who stood at a white and clean stove, doing something.

Just now she was cracking his eggs into the pan and as they fell they began to sputter, lowly; which pleased him, as the morning itself pleased him, and after he had sat and drunk off two glasses of milk he expelled his breath: "Ah!" It was only after this that there came from the stove his wife's asking, how he had slept, then? Why, he had slept fine, good. And then, but not right away, she observed, that it was a nice morning. A good morning — Pepicelli thought so too, and said so; which led Kate, serving him now, to say what a good summer it had been all along, and why didn't he look at the paper she had set there, for him; so he did, and they talked about what the paper said. She said she had some screens she wished he would paint and he answered, he would do it. When time came for him to go she gave him his jacket and said she would see him, then, for supper, and here was his lunchbox.

Pepicelli came off the back steps and looked toward the motorcycle. It was partly concealed behind the shoulder of the house, its body hooded by the canvas. He thought to himself, so, his new property, his machine, it was still there. He would go and see what the night had done to it.

He crumpled back the half-stiff canvas. There was the cycle, supporting herself between the fence and the side of the house, her metal cold to the hands, her sable paint dulled in the morning damp. She had a large chromium-plated headlight, dull-silvered now, shaped like the half of a great pearl, mounted upon her forehead above her handlebars; when he stroked it to wipe away the mist the morning flashed out suddenly brightly from it, startling him a little, and he saw his hand, grotesquely swollen, tapering down to be a part of a tiny squat Pepicelli. For a moment then he looked at her, just looked, and then he told himself she would be all right where she was, and he retucked the canvas around her.

A door slammed in the next house. Pepicelli strode out into the yard. Nick came shuffling down his own back steps. Pepicelli called, "Hey!" Nick, heading for his garage, looked over and called back, "Hey! You ready? Get out there!"

"Sure, Nick," said Pepicelli. He walked out front, and the two of them drove to work.

Pepicelli had always liked working in the long summers. But today it bothered him somehow just having to be there, and before the sun had risen even to noon he had considered it might be a good thing to go home early and inspect the thing — look her over good

— that he had picked up the day before.

So he caught an early bus. By midafternoon he was back at the house. His wife was out shopping or somewhere. He went down to the cycle and rolled her with him, stepping backwards, out onto the grass. He stood her up there, placing a wooden chock between her kickstand and the soft ground.

She stood free on the grass, her front wheel nodded slightly with the lean of her to one side, the sunlight glinting in her finish, flashing circular from her silvered rims and headlight, and to Pepicelli it seemed incredible, the way she showed herself so well, standing clear: how long she was, her body thick-made, heavy, but rounded and containing herself, which showed you something of her strength, right there; how her tank, shining black, bulged out above her engine on both sides before the saddle, like strong hunched-up shoulders, and she thinned back behind to just the rounded fender, rounded with the glimmering rim. But her motor, that was the heart of her really, her power, just as it was with a car; and how she carried it, a drab piece of stained steel, cylinder-abutted, infested with innumerable wires, bound around with gauges, carburetor, generator, battery: how she carried it, beneath her body yet part of her, rounding her lines about it, unapologetic so to speak, proving that it was not ugly, no more than the rest of her, massed there in its power while the sparkplug caps glittered like metallic stones in the sunlight.

Pepicelli got a cloth and then he went all over

her, rubbing and cleaning, wiping away what bits of dirt and grease he could find. With his hands he felt each of the tires for hardness. He traced a few wires, but for the most part touched the motor gingerly. He looked at the rocker clutch, and standing by the handlebars he worked the accelerator a little and squeezed the handbrakes a few times. The shift looked all right. He tried the saddle-springs once, twice, with his hand and told himself they seemed all right, too. He walked around the machine again and again, feeling there was something more to be done and trying to find it, eventually re-doing all the things he had done already until, later, his wife appeared upstairs on the back porch, and looking him straight in the face, almost so as not to see what he was about, called:

"It's ready! You going to come?"

"Sure," said Pepicelli. "Right now." And he wheeled the cycle back to her place between the fence and the house-siding, and wrapped her again in her canvas.

The next two days went very much the same. Pepicelli was up early, and coming out of the house went over to the motorcycle to see how she had weathered the night. By the middle of the afternoon he was home again, and the cycle was standing free in the backyard.

On the third day Pepicelli was again late for supper. But Kate didn't worry, as he had told her he would be seeing the agent about the house. When he came home and didn't say anything Kate wanted to know, what about it? He had seen him, Pepicelli said. Well, and what? He would have to go back, Pepicelli said.

After supper they sat in the living room. Pepicelli read the newspaper, but he fidgeted and changed from one page to another. Kate didn't notice. Tonight it was she who was tired, and she went off to bed early. She fell asleep quickly.

By that time Pepicelli was no longer in the house even, but standing in the dark in the backyard. For a moment he stood there, until he could see better; then he went over to the side of the house. His two hands grasped the canvas covering the motorcycle and carefully drew it from her. There she was, large and dark beside him so that he could scarcely make her out, but against his leg he could feel the rough abutments of the motor and higher, the smoothness of the tank. The metal of the tank was cool. With a sudden groping he found the handlegrips, and swinging a thick leg across her fender was suddenly up in the saddle. Pepicelli: how he felt the size and power of her swelling under him then; his legs wide-straddling the great motor, fitting tightly into her frame as they should, his feet finding naturally where they belonged, close-ready on the brake and clutch, while he seemed to hold all her power, everything, tight in control with his strong clasp upon her handlegrips. He moved up forward on her, pressed his knees against the tank as if for a jump, settled back, raised himself easily in the saddle and then came down upon it, bouncing, but none too lightly, in his seat. The springs made a noise. Pepicelli heard it, and somehow it struck him; everything he had been feeling began to pass out of him. He almost thought he felt ashamed. There was no other sound. The cycle was quiet and immobile under him. Without saying so to himself Pepicelli knew it was nothing at all like it had been in the park. After sitting there quietly for a short time he drew the canvas back over the machine and went into the house.

  He did not sleep, though he went straight to bed. And the next day, although he remained for the full time at the park because, as he told himself, he had been going home early too many times lately, he did not do much work either — hardly any at all.

  When at supper he took nothing but a cup of strong coffee, his wife said to eat, what was the matter? Pepicelli answered, never mind about it, he wasn't hungry. Yes, the heat, his wife said, it was getting hot all of a sudden, the heat was coming. "Who said, heat!" Pepicelli burst out. He wasn't hungry, that's what he'd said. He shoved his cup into the middle of the table, announcing, "I've had mine!" Then he pushed and kicked his way out through the screen door.

  Down below there was no pause or hesitation. Pepicelli pulled off the tarpaulin, laid it over the fence unfolded, backed the big motorcycle out to where she could turn round; and then the two of them, Pepicelli walking deliberately, conducting the cycle by her saddle and one handlegrip, passed out the driveway into the road. Across the street three little girls were playing jump-rope, two of them twirling, the rope splat-splatting, the other girl, who lived across there somewhere, hopping, breathless, counting; when there appeared coming out the driveway opposite her a man pushing something, how big it was! and she missed. The rope stopped, and so did the game; she ran across to see the thing and watch the man, who was bending over it, looking, touching, like he was getting ready to do something; and he wouldn't look at her or the other two girls who came over, didn't he see them? But she knew who he was now and she asked, "Whose is that, Mr. Pepicelli? Where did you get that?"

Pepicelli said nothing. He straightened up, very carefully mounted to the saddle, and balanced the machine the best he could with one foot on the curb. His eyes were intent upon the ignition, the gauges, the pedals where his feet should place themselves; they fixed finally on the kick starter. He cocked his leg and brought the heel of his work shoe up to it. The little girls watched him. And now there were more than the three girls, bicycles racing up, one, then more, skid-whistling, stopping in a cluster around the motorcycle, kids' voices talking to Pepicelli, to one another, one of them yelling, "Art! Hey, Art! Here! Come on!" More people came along to look on, and not only children: men with lunchboxes and the evening newspaper, a woman from a nearby house, standing on the sidewalk to watch the thick little black-haired man, Mr. Pepicelli, who was sitting on a motorcycle and — there! — he kicked at something. Pepicelli, in the saddle, felt the starter kick back at him, doubling back his leg almost so hard as to throw him, and he had to dismount for a look. People wondered. More of them crowded up, men in neckties, draftsmen perhaps, a woman or two with a shopping bag, a young girl and with her a young fellow — just a kid, red-headed, very freckled, extremely tall, who could see over the necessary heads without much trouble. He saw the motorcycle and was in an instant standing in the road beside the squat Pepicelli, whom he drew back a little from the machine. He threw a gangling leg of his own over her, and was in the saddle. And then, everybody watching, he rose above them all, incredibly high, in the air; his red head came down flashing, and with it a clap of thunder, deafening, and then rolling along the street, bouncing against the house-faces, filling the valley of houses that was Third Street.

The roar shoved back the bystanders, cleared away the bicycles, and the young man sat the machine in a little space, rolling her sound with a thin wrist that was freckled and jeweled with a silver wristwatch. He grinned at the people watching and then tried to say something to Pepicelli, who had not moved from beside the motorcycle, but nobody could make it out above the noise. "All right! All right!" Pepicelli could be heard shouting harshly. "Get off of her!" The young man went back to stand by his girl, who smiled at him, just a little smile, while Pepicelli mounted once again.

Pepicelli: how he felt it all then, the real power

of her, pounding and harsh, but fluctuating into infinite nuance within where her pistons moved unseen and strong; how he felt her throbbing unbelievably between his knees, vibrating the very air, filling his ears, and hammering there; shocking her strength into him through his arms, responding to his heavy throttle hand with a force that was almost fearful to him! What might she do? He must know; she must run; urge her to it, to her utmost swiftness, as hard as she would ride; conquer everything, roads, hills, wherever she might carry him. He had known horses, but she was somehow bigger, and more beautiful; he had seen her run. And now he was on her, she roaring under him, ready, and everybody giving her room like a rearing animal!

Faces swam up to windows, front doors came open, people stepped onto porches. What was it, the police? No, that man lives around here. Right across the way. Pepicelli. What's he doing on that thing? He must be almost fifty. Looks good on her though, don't he. Like kid. Where's his wife? She's the one who ought to see him.

Looking out through her summer curtains, Kate saw everything well enough. She told herself that she was disgusted. The sound of the motorcycle, filling the room, became even louder for a moment. Outside she could see Pepicelli, sitting up sturdy and straight, move out from the curb in tentative jerks and bucks to go on slowly down the street. He came back more smoothly, but not too fast, and the bicycles got out of the way to let him pass. But the third time she heard the sound raising pitch while still far away, expanding as it came, until the sound, the rush, Pepicelli unbentover in the wind, swept at once through the street and away, out of sight and at last of hearing, altogether. When he did not make another pass people began to go home.

 Kate waited. She waited until after midnight but then it was late, so she went to bed. She waited all through the next day. On the days following she called people. She called everybody she could think of. Somebody told old Brennan about it and he laughed and said, maybe he'd have her come back and keep his house. But within a few weeks Kate had moved in with her brother and sister-in-law, and none of them ever heard of Pepicelli again.

John Sobieski Runs

John Sobieski Runs

One September afternoon the door of the cross-country team room at an upstate New York high school opened a little way and then closed again, admitting in that instant a very short boy who looked a little underfed, even for his size. Nobody paid him the least attention. In the first place, there were only three people in the room. One was a member of the varsity, a dark Italian-looking boy dressed ready to go out in sweatpants and a sweatshirt with a picture of a winged spiked shoe printed in red on its breast. He sat tying on his lightweight cross-country shoes in front of a locker sky blue in color and spangled with white stars, with a white-and-red stripe running around its edges. Most of the lockers were dark green, but there were half a dozen such colorful ones. The dark boy sat on one of two wooden benches running the length of the room about two feet out from the lockers. On the opposite bench a boy in track shorts lay stomach down, his head to one side, arms hanging, while a serious-faced young man, an assistant coach, picked with his fingers very fast at the backs of the other's legs, snick-snick-snick-snick-snick. The liniment he was using smelled sharply above the prevailing, long-accumulated odor of sweat.

Turning from the door the short boy stepped over one of the benches in a motion remarkably easy, considering his size. With his face in the corner made by the last locker and the wall, he began to undress. He had with him a blue looseleaf notebook, which he laid on the bench. Then he took off a brown knit sweater and folded that on top of the notebook. Underneath he was wearing a white shirt starched so stiffly that when he took it off it held the creases of his wearing and would only fold brokenly in a high springy pile. Now he stood for a moment in his undershirt, with slender shoulders and brown hair about the color of his sweater, wearing a pair of darker brown pants. He looked as though he had been sent to the corner for something he ought to be ashamed of. He had been trying to get something out of his pocket that didn't want to come, but all at once, as he stood tugging, the thing flew out — an ordinary piece of blue cloth — with a sweep and flourish that seemed to disconcert him. Immediately he loosened his belt and let his trousers fall to his ankles. He stepped out of them and into the blue cloth thing, a cheap pair of gym shorts with a string pull at the waist. These on, he was uniformed. He rolled up his pants at the top of his little pile, bent and tightened the strings of his shoes and, fixing his eyes on the door at the far end of the room, walked toward it between the rows of lockers, a very thin boy who might have been called lanky if he had been a foot taller. He opened the door, looked out, and finding that it led to the playing field, disappeared through it, running.

In the locker room the varsity member, his dark hair hanging over his face in long Vaselined strands, had finished with his running shoes. With a shake he laid his hair back on his head in orderly lines and at the same time gave one single, sophisticated glance across at his coach.

The serious-faced young man said only, "He could grow," and continued picking.

John Sobieski — this was the short boy's name — found himself running out of the school building's shadow into the warm sunlight, over hard even ground covered with short grass which stretched away, from beneath his own thin legs, into the biggest flat field he had ever seen. Moving across it, he passed over gleaming lines of white lime powder and except for them did not feel he was moving at all, running though he was across the big green field in the sun. He saw, far away on his left, the football players, tiny bright-colored people, hunching and waiting, rising and moving and entangling all together in waves; heard whistles; and saw before him, past many lines and various goalposts, more boys — the running team. Many were lying all about on the ground, but many were standing up too, all upright together in a tight kind of pack that vibrated and moved around like a thing in itself, something very bright, red and white, spinning there in the sunshine on top of uncountable bare legs. As he came nearer he saw that the people on the ground were only discarded sweatsuits with nobody in them; the runners were all up and gathered around a very tall man who was waving a clipboard of papers in the air above his head as he spoke. The runners had on bright red shirts with lettering across the chest and white shorts edged in red, and they shifted and pranced on their slight little running shoes as on hooves, their bright uniforms blended and mingled to make up that whirling bright-colored thing which, idling nervous and impatient in place up until now, suddenly lurched and flexed and strained within before extending itself loosely and easily away as, on its many legs, it began trotting off over the field. John Sobieski ran as hard as he knew how; as he pounded up, the big man flagged him on with the paper-fluttering clipboard, boomed, "Right there....after those men!" and John Sobieski was past and pounding after the pack of runners that stretched away loose and red and white in the sunlight toward a far fence bordering the field.

So they were running, and John Sobieski was with them. But already his legs felt heavy and he was breathing faster than he had ever breathed in his life. He had come running all the way across the big green field only to find that they had started already. The unfairness of it made him hot and sick. He had come

John Sobieski Runs

out for cross-country knowing he would have to run miles, but they had started before he was ready. His throat ached; his feet he raised up and clapped down like flatirons. As he ran he thought to himself, "It's not my fault, they started before I was ready....I'll stop right up here somewhere."

They had come to the end of the field and passed through a gate; they were running on a sidewalk past houses. A boy in a red shirt was running not far in front of him. John Sobieski could see his own shoes hitting the sidewalk one after the other, while he himself seemed to ride up above somewhere as on some funny kind of running machine. Bumping along in this way he was interested to find, after a while, that his machine seemed to be moving a little faster than the other boy's machine. Fascinated, with curiosity and detachment mixed, he watched the increasing nearness of the other boy's white pants — for some reason that was all he could see — until gradually he came alongside the other. Both of them were bouncing up and down furiously, but the other boy seemed to bounce up and down in the same spot while John Sobieski was very slowly moving until, gradually again, he couldn't see the other boy anymore. But it didn't make any difference, there was another one in front of him.

And this one approached and went by, and another one sprang up. Regular as telephone poles they went slowly by him until there had been six. He counted them because he didn't have anything else to do. Then everything grew dark, and though it was only because they had entered a park and were running on a path through woods, John Sobieski didn't know it. All he knew was that he was running after a strange white flag that moved before him in the dim. Fluttering and twinkling always ahead it dipped and wound with the path, and John Sobieski behind. At last, after a long time, they broke out into the sunlight. There was the fence around the shadowed green playing field and inside it the football players looking weary in their dirtied uniforms and beyond them, far across the field, the high school building. John Sobieski's heart lifted. He saw that the white flag was nothing but another pair of the white shorts edged with red, the boy running in them was only strides in front, and though he was tired he set himself to beat this one boy at least. As he sprinted around the fence toward the school — which burned at its edges like a coal, blocking off the sun — it seemed to him he had only just started, he was virtually flying, he would pass them all. And he did overtake the boy in the twinkling white pants, and another.

Standing up against the bricks of the school building the assistant coach, who had just finished a rubdown in the locker room, watched the line of long-distance runners coming around the fence. They toiled with incredible slowness and suffering, each one preserving only the formal attitude of running. Long ago they had lost the speed the attitude is supposed to produce. He watched them toiling, one by one, and as he watched, one moving slightly faster than the rest strained painfully closer to the next man, painfully abreast, and in time came up behind the next runner, whom he would probably pass before reaching the school. The coach turned and walked swiftly toward a corner of the building.

Now the leaders had reached a gate by the school. There something halted them, making them run into one another in their weariness. As John Sobieski came up he stumbled and fell against the slippery neck of the boy in front of him. The boy's sweat came away on his lips, and as they passed through the gate a man shouted something at each one. John Sobieski felt his shoulder grabbed and squeezed.

"Thirteen!" said the man to him. It was the assistant coach.

Nobody was running anymore. They all walked around in circles. So did John Sobieski. He felt sick again. His chest and throat exploded every time he tried to breathe, and he was terribly hot. What he wanted most was just to be unconscious, but he couldn't bear to sit or lie down. He saw a boy crouching on the ground, retching onto the grass between his hands. Somebody had brought in the sweatclothes off the playing field and boys were picking their own out of a pile. They hung their sweatshirts over their shoulders like capes and tied the arms in front. After a while John Sobieski began to feel better. He walked toward the locker room more or less with five other runners. Just in front walked the boy who had vomited, with a friend supporting him on either side. A sweatshirt was thrown across John Sobieski's shoulders; the arms came dangling down in front of him. He never saw who did it because nobody seemed to look at him or pay much attention to him.

Back in the locker room it was strangely quiet considering the place was filling with runners, who sat down on the benches or tinkered quietly at their locker doors. John Sobieski went to his own pile of things, turned his back and let his blue shorts slide down to his shoes. Holding his brown pants open he stepped into them, stuffed the shorts into his pocket, pulled the crackling white shirt over his undershirt and the sweater over that; and leaving the sweatshirt neatly folded on the bench he turned around and stood, his back to the entrance door, surveying the room. It was if he had only just come in and was looking for something. Now he smelled the perspiration smell fresh and strong and moist, mingling with the steam that clouded out from the top of the shower-room door and mingling, too, with all the hubbub that had come up in the short time he was changing. Everybody in the steamy room seemed naked and they all seemed unnaturally up above him, but that was only because nearly all the runners by now were standing on the two benches, which were two parallel pedestals for their sweating, moving nude bodies. John Sobieski moved between them in his brown sweater, looking very intently for something, and having no attention paid him. He even walked a little way into the shower room, clothes and shoes on and all, and peered through the steam at the runners there. But nobody seemed to notice this either.

Finally he went out the same door he had first come in by, passed through a few halls, and left the building.

"Thirty-four," he said to himself as he stepped outside into the cold afternoon air. "I beat twenty-one at least."

He walked home. The night passed, and then the next day — but John Sobieski couldn't have said how. He was a small thin boy sitting at back desks in various classrooms with a blue notebook open in front of him, but what he was seeing was not a teacher or a blackboard, but four or five boys in twinkling white pants running before him and he himself coming up behind, planning how he was going to take them.

By four in the afternoon he was on the field again. The runners were warming up. Some were doing pushups; some were lying on their backs on the damp ground and springing up in quick little sitting motions; some just stood around with serious faces, paying no attention to others; some were rotating their torsos, with hands on hips. John Sobieski looked around carefully and did some of the same things. The tall man of the day before was nowhere to be seen, but after a few minutes the assistant coach came walking out toward them with a boy on either side. His face was hard and dark, but his eyes were large and white and serious and appeared to be considering other things even as he said something brief and imperative to the boy next to him. This boy gave a single vigorous nod and without warning whirled, and was away. Instantly the others took after him and John Sobieski, who hadn't been ready for it to happen so fast, was left doing pushups on the ground.

    He jumped up and ran after them, though he knew it was hopeless; he was already fifty yards behind the pack and at least a hundred behind the leaders. For the second time they had started before he was ready. Before they had even left the playing field he felt sicker than at any time the previous day. His body was a misery to him. He ran beside the endless steel wire fence crying to himself, "Why did I think I could run? I can't!" He ran another hundred yards and then prayed, "Please let me just finish. I don't want to beat anybody. All I want to do is finish." Because somewhere inside him was the idea that if he could just endure it this one time he might get a fair chance, when he could really do something, tomorrow.

    His father had warned him. At the end of the summer, when John Sobieski came home one night and told his mother and father that he wasn't going back to St. Stephen's any more but was going up to the high school, his father had said to him, "What do you think you'll get by going up there?"

"You can do what you want when you get out," the boy answered. "You can be what you want."

His father, smoking, muttered something to himself while he shook out a long wooden match. "Nah — you can't do what you want," he said then, and blew out smoke. "You just try it, John Sobieski, and you'll find out. Just stay where you are."

"No, I'm going up there."

Then his father looked straight at him. Something ugly came into his look. "Do you know who you are?"

"Everybody knows who they are."

"No they don't. But you — you're John Sobieski. That was my father's name. He came over here when he wasn't any bigger than you are now. He and some others were the ones that built St. Stephen's in the old days. That's where you belong, right around here. No use going anywhere different because you ain't ever going to be any different from that."

"Yes I am," said John Sobieski. "Oh yes I am."

They looked at each other, the two of them almost exactly the same size except that everything about the father was somehow thicker and more unwieldy. They looked at one another from opposing chairs until John Sobieski's father's expression broke, and he turned away.

"You think you can do what you want," he said. "You start out all right with it too. You leave the house every morning and you only come back at night. You get pretty far away. After awhile you think you don't have to come back at all. Then one day you get caught out there all by yourself — and you get licked good."

"You talk like that because you're old," said John Sobieski. "I'm not old. Why should I listen to it?"

Struggling, spreading out, the runners pounded along upon a hard city sidewalk. They strained and reached, with knees and toes and shoulders. Each step had only one purpose — to slide over as much ground as possible. Most of them could not see, and none paid any attention to the big car that followed along in the street keeping pace, but inside it the head coach, the tall man who usually carried the clipboard thick with papers, hovered just beyond the toil of the runners. Ahead of him in the next block he watched an indistinct cluster of legs and a flash of color separate themselves, as he came closer, into a runner in blue shorts and white top trailing a line of three abreast in the red-and-white uniforms. As blue-and-white closed with the red the legs became entangled and inextricable again, until suddenly somebody got stepped on. A boy in red shirt and white pants reeled to the side, off the curb and onto the road where he fought to recover himself, climbing back to the sidewalk only to drop rapidly to the rear, his pace broken. Meantime blue-and-white had moved up between the other two so that the three of them, bouncing up and down, remained for a long moment like a slot machine come to rest after changing, red-blue-red, until gradually blue-and-white disengaged himself again and moved out in front.

John Sobieski Runs

The coach accelerated and passed on, but John Sobieski didn't see him. He had hardly even seen the three runners. His eyes were wet and partly closed as he ran, and all at once he knew that something was in front of him, preventing him. More or less, he saw them. But there wasn't anything he could do except keep running, because he knew if he were checked at all he would have to stop altogether. Then after a moment he was clear and by himself again. He ran on. No vision of the school building raised him. It was a gray, damp day. He didn't know how far they still had to go. He passed more runners, singles or straggling twos, without any struggle. He couldn't think about taking them, or anything; they were just going slower than he was, and he moved by.

It was over abruptly. They passed through the same gate as yesterday freely, without being stopped, the runners all streaming in and dispersing, and as soon as John Sobieski realized where they were and stopped trying to run he collapsed.

"Walk him around!" somebody shouted. It was the tall head coach. He had parked his car and now stood just inside the gate, wearing a long raincoat. "What's the trouble?"

Two runners had already lifted John Sobieski to his feet, but he was fighting them off and they couldn't hold him; they were tired themselves.

"He's talking to himself," one answered between breaths. "He's trying to say numbers."

"Walk him around," the tall man repeated. "That's the way to finish a run. There isn't a one of you that should have anything left at all."

The two of them took John Sobieski's arms across their shoulders and together they walked him around on the grass. After a while they had their own wind back, but as soon as John Sobieski got wind enough he began to cough. The afternoon was chilly and damp. He took several wheezing breaths and then coughed again, badly. By the time the others had walked off the effects of their run, he was coughing steadily for long stretches.

The two boys took him into the locker room. They sat him on a bench in front of their own lockers and got his clothes off, while he continued coughing. They walked him with care through the jostling, sweating, strong-smelling runners into the steamy shower room and one readied a shower while the other held John Sobieski. Then they put him under it and left him.

Later, when the two runners were dressed and ready to leave, they turned to find the small thin boy standing naked across the bench from them, dripping onto the floor.

"Feel better now?" the bigger one asked. "What's the matter, forget your towel?" He drew his own heavy damp one from his gym bag and took the one that his friend was carrying rolled up under one arm and hung them both over John Sobieski's shoulders. The small boy opened his mouth to say something but instead he

was overcome by a fit of coughing.
 The two had to go. "Give them to us tomorrow," said the one, pausing in the locker room door. He was a big, strong-looking boy with a very large head. "Ernest Borkmann and Joe Felice." Still John Sobieski stood looking at the two boys; he was fighting a rising cough and the door had already closed before he called after them:
 "John Sobieski!"
 He went back to the bench with his towels. He wiped himself, put on his clothes and put his running shorts in his pocket. He took the towels along home with him. His second day's running was over.
 When he reached his own street it was dark and a cold foggy rain was drifting down. By the light of streetlights the wooden two-family houses rose high all around him, their thrusting peaked roofs shoulder to shoulder, the mist falling from the darkness above upon their wet slate backs. Inside they were warmly lighted behind curtains.
 John Sobieski went straight to his bedroom. His mother and father could hear him coughing behind the door. Finally he came out and sat down at the table. A fire was going in the kitchen stove, since it was early in the year to light the furnace, and in the sudden close warmth John Sobieski began to perspire and then to cough and cough. His eyes would become fixed, his face red and contorted as he tried to stop himself, at least long enough to eat; but the thing would burst out

at last and leave him shaking, his eyes watering. He drank cups and cups of coffee, which his mother poured out for him. His father read a newspaper on the other side of the table and glanced at John Sobieski when he coughed, but said nothing.

Later, as he sat on the sofa in the living room, wearing his heavy sweater, his cough subsided. His mother and his father sat across from him on either side in upholstered chairs; his mother's fingers were crocheting something nimbly, and his father still had his paper. John Sobieski sat by himself on the sofa doing nothing, thinking about nothing, just sitting still under a lamp and gazing blankly at his parents. At one point, as his father folded over his paper to study the lower corner, he caught his son gazing at him.

"What now?"

"Nothing. Can't I look?"

His mother, too, raised her head, worried-looking and sorrowful. She reminded John Sobieski of those old women with kerchiefs around their heads whom he would see when he had been an altar boy serving early mass. They knelt and prayed, holding their beads, with a look upon their faces and in their eyes as though the whole world were filled with sorrow; and John Sobieski hated sorrow, he couldn't stand it.

"I don't like that coughing," said his mother, shaking her head.

But John Sobieski didn't mind even sorrow, now. All he wanted was just to sit as he was, in his own house, doing nothing, thinking about nothing at all.

   Then morning came again, and John Sobieski must go up to the high school. He took the two towels plus a third one for himself from his mother, his running shorts, his notebook, his lunch bag and a black umbrella of his father's because the morning was dark and threatening rain again. By the time he reached the school his arms ached from carrying so many things, and when he thought of the running he would have to do that day he felt sorry for himself and thought, "No wonder I can't run. Nobody else has to wear themselves out just getting here."
   The rain in clinging drops or running down the panes of the windows, the shifting light and dark places in the sky — all were watched apprehensively by John Sobieski as he sat in the classrooms' dim electric light that could barely establish itself all day against the bleak light from outside. After his last class, as he walked among crowds of others through the dim and noisy corridors, Ernest Borkmann found him.
   The big boy took him down to the wing of the school where the lockers were, past the door of the cross-country room and on to a further door where he left him. For a moment John Sobieski hesitated, but then he let himself inside quickly and faced the room.
   In front of him, behind a desk, sat the tall man of the clipboard — a large and handsome-appearing man with long white hair combed back, seen now for the

first time indoors without coat and hat. Leaning back with folded hands, he was talking to the smaller, darker, bony-looking young man who sat on the windowsill with his back to the rain, his knees drawn up high and his feet on the radiator.

"Is that him?" the tall man asked. "The one that runs in the blue pants?"

The other coach nodded gloomily, watching John Sobieski, the whites of his eyes showing in his dark face.

"What do they call him, anyway?"

A little smile hung at the corners of the white-haired man's eyes and lips, as though to him things were always cheerful and even, somehow, funny.

"John Sobieski," responded the boy himself.

"John Sobieski.....I hear John Sobieski's a pretty good runner, Stan."

"He does the best he can."

"No sir," said the white-haired man, "he likes to run. He likes to go out there and beat those other boys. He likes to take 'em. How is he going to do it the way he's been, Stanley? It isn't right. We have to give John Sobieski a chance, the same as everybody else. You come here, John Sobieski."

The tall man reached forward and pointed to a box at the front of his desk. Of course it had been there all along, but for John Sobieski it only came into being at that moment. The boy opened it. Inside, under tissue paper, his hands grasped a pair of the spikeless cross-country shoes.

John Sobieski Runs

He lifted them out. They were small in size, for his own little feet, narrow and light and pointed, with hard and sharp rubber bottoms for digging in and starting; and he could see himself already, as from some distance away, the black shoes slashing like hooves, slashing and slashing in arcs, the shoes of John Sobieski!

"John Sobieski's going to Utica with us," said the head coach, grinning. "John Sobieski's going to run in Syracuse. John Sobieski's going to New York City."

"You get a uniform and sweatshirt from the manager, John Sobieski," the younger man told him more soberly. "Put a towel around your neck when you go outside. And don't try to run very hard today. It's too cold for it."

The runners jogged across the field and gathered together under the drizzling clouds. Neither coach was anywhere around. John Sobieski had been one of the first ones out and for once, at least, he was ready. Imperceptibly this time, without a signal of any kind, the runners began their run. They moved off slowly without making any sound, all the move and flash of their bright uniforms muffled within the heavy gray sweatsuits. They moved at a shuffle just over a walk, then at a trot, and then a little better. In the beginning they ran very close to one another in a tight pack, and yet in rigid silence, as though pushing together against some enormous burden, one so heavy that it might never be moved at all without an effort from each so intense as to isolate him from all the others.

Once outside the fence John Sobieski found the pack lengthening. As it stretched out gradually it seemed to snap in two. He was the last of the line that was moving ahead, and there were nine runners in front of him. He stayed where he was without working very hard. Then all at once, when he was scarcely tired, he spied the school building ahead of him and he pulled out and ran as fast as he could. He passed the others easily, every one — not so fast as if they were standing still, but as if he were moving about twice as fast — and entered the gate first by a long interval.

Instead of stopping he kept running straight on into the locker room. There he took a hurried shower and had already dried himself by the time the others had begun to come in, talking quietly, in twos and threes. John Sobieski dressed as fast as he could, his face buried in the new locker that had been assigned to him. He was afraid to turn around because they might all be looking at him, because he had come in first. He felt as though he were charged with electricity and the figure "1" were shining out upon his back.

He was sweating again by the time he reached home. His coughing was so continuous that he knew he would not be able to stop it or even halt it for a few minutes until he had something to drink. Even so, he went directly to his bedroom and carefully spread out on the bed his new running things, which were now all wrinkled and damp. The unfamiliar bright-colored things

John Sobieski Runs

attracted his mother and father, who came in to look.

"Where can I put these to dry," John Sobieski began, but then he closed his eyes, grasping the long bar at the foot of his bed; his upper body leaned forward, the tears pressed against his shut eyes and the cough came rolling out of him, "where nobody will touch them?"

"Touch them," said his father. "What are we going to touch them for?"

"We can hang them up over the stove," his mother assured him with bright, grieving eyes that made the boy furious. "Come and eat supper."

"I'll be there!" he said. "I have to see about this stuff first."

It was Friday night. John Sobieski had the whole weekend to dry his running outfit, and on Monday he went to the school equipped like all the others — except that he had come in first the last time they had run. But that same day the figure "1," which he could almost feel burning upon his back once he was among the runners again, faded out. Nobody paid any attention to it.

Now every day was bright and blue. The cold air burned like alcohol on the skin of his arms and legs when he took off his sweatclothes and began to run in the afternoons. He was happy just to run with the others, keeping up with them along different streets of the city that he had not known anything about before. In the first time trials he finished twelfth.

John Sobieski Runs

The coaches took fifteen boys to run at Utica the following Saturday. They drove a few hours in cars, got out to warm up behind a strange and brand-new high school, gathered on a line in a bunch — one of a dozen such, each in its own bright colors — and then a gun was fired, a cloud of white smoke rose above the man who had fired it, and the bunches all sprang into a forward wave to cross the field together. John Sobieski was left behind, exhausted, right at the start. He decided that he would finish the race this one last time, and then he would never run again. He felt that way all through the unfamiliar woods and as he came down out of them onto the field again, into the mouth of the bullpen between funneling ropes that crowded him against boys in front and on both sides until he stood still with one of the coarse-fibered ropes in either hand. Somebody wrote something on his back — a piece of paper with a number on it had been pinned to his red shirt — and then he staggered away, to walk around and begin coughing.

Riding home in the head coach's car, he learned that their team had won the meet. Their first five men had come in 2nd, 4th, 5th, 7th and 8th for a score of 26. John Sobieski found the number 24 written in pencil underneath the big printed number he had torn from his back. Besides, he had a blue satin ribbon. Two hundred boys had run, but only the first twenty-five received ribbons.

On Monday his name was in the morning newspaper. "A freshman, John Sobieski, was the Red and White's tenth finisher." Ernest Borkmann had cut the story out of the paper and showed it to him in the locker room before practice.

"Where did you come in?" John Sobieski asked him.

The big boy folded the clipping carefully with large strong fingers and put it away in his wallet. "I got sick," he answered, frowning. "I didn't finish."

Saturday they ran at Syracuse, and there were twice as many runners. The high school placed second. John Sobieski, their seventh man in, finished 39th. It meant he had improved about nine places. And he beat three of their own runners who had finished ahead of him the week before.

This time he rode home with the younger coach. The other runners were subdued; John Sobieski's coughing was louder than all their quiet talk. It filled the car, though he strained to suppress it by sitting motionless with all the air breathed out of him, so that he would have nothing to cough with. But he had to breathe again sometime and then the air would rush into his lungs, explode, and be thrown out once more. "Roll up your windows," the coach told the runners. Twice they stopped at gas stations to let him drink water, but even so he would start coughing again in a few minutes.

Now John Sobieski noticed that boys on the running team spoke to him when he saw them in the school's halls, and even some others seemed to know who he was. He lived only for running. He got up in the morning and walked to the school for it, waiting all day for that living half hour when he emerged on the playing field and ran, suffering, until he swore he would never do it again and at last finished somehow and returned to the locker room. His life was running. It was different now than ever before. "I only eat and sleep at home," he thought to himself as he sat and watched his father and mother in the evening. "They see me go away, and they see me come back. But they don't know what I do."

It was five o'clock in the morning. New York City, the biggest city in America, lay more than a hundred and fifty miles away to the east and south. The head coach had already driven off with five boys, and now the younger coach and two remaining runners and a manager all got into a little car that stood by itself at the curb in front of the school. John Sobieski had the front seat. He hunched down inert and from there watched the dark houses, the peaking rooftops, roll by. Nobody said anything. The manager and the runner in the back seat were trying to sleep. Once they were well into the country, John Sobieski sat up and looked out. It was just getting light. The sky was gray, as though cloudy. In the open fields there was light, but everything else remained shadowy. Buildings that they passed stood gray and chill-appearing, except for yellow windows distinct and square in a few isolated houses. The boy was glad to see them. It struck him as cheerful somehow, for it meant that people were awake within and beginning their work for the day. Something in him yearned toward them, but he was going to New York City; and he was glad to be going to New York, but he didn't want to run there.

The next time he looked out it was fully light; the day would be clear. They were driving on a parkway now, twin concrete highways that descended endlessly taking huge dips and turns. As the car rose up with engine roaring to meet each new crest, John Sobieski waited to see if the city were ahead, but the road on the other side only plunged them downhill again, twisting out of sight among hills and woods. He couldn't sleep, but he closed his eyes for a long, long time hoping that when he opened them again they would be there and he would at least have rested a little.

What made him sit up again finally was a loud whining of tires. Then outside, all around, he saw more cars, a great many of them all going to the same place. The young coach sitting next to him was very busy driving. John Sobieski saw that the man's face was now intent, his eyes fiercely concentrated ahead. He was passing the other cars as though they were runners. They went between some fairly high buildings and then ran downhill across a bridge; the coach paid money out his window, they went on down the ramp, blue water came round on the right, and immediately up in front of them, very high, a suspension bridge swung across to the other side. They drove underneath it, and there were the tall buildings of New York standing out as he had thought they would be — except that they weren't down close to the water but were built on a hill rising to the left.

Just then the runner in the back seat — it was the same dark-haired boy who had been sitting on the bench when John Sobieski first entered the locker room — called out, "Hey, we're on the island!"

The older runner knew they should be running at a park somewhere back in the Bronx. The coach knew it too — he had run there himself as a cross-country runner — but coming into the city he had missed his turn and was still looking for it when he had been caught among the cars rushing into Manhattan. He got off the parkway now and they ran steeply uphill between buildings, all of them bigger than John Sobieski had ever seen, but not what he had expected of New York either. They were big dirty boxes with innumerable windows in which, it looked like, people lived. It gave him a pang to think that.

They kept turning into different streets, driving fast, and then they were out of Manhattan again. All at once the coach turned off the highway and drove straight across a flat athletic field. Right where he stopped the car the runners were massed — bright colored, moving and shifting by the hundreds, tightening up — and just as they went to get out a shot was fired. The pack jolted, loosened and stretched away like an expanding accordion, the farther edge moving rapidly over the field while the near edge remained on the starting line playing out runners in waves. The coach swore aloud as he helped to rip jackets and sweatclothes from John Sobieski and the other runner. Then the two of them were on the field running, before some had even left the starting line.

And if ever they had started before John Sobieski was ready, it was this time. Next to him, in front of him, behind him, shoving him, were runners; and he himself, short and thin, unable even to see above them. As a drowning man sees his entire life, he saw his running: he knew he couldn't run, he was always sick, he only beat others by torturing himself. And he hated it because he cared only about beating the others and not all of them either, but mostly those on his own team, for of the rest there were so many as to make his struggles seem indistinguishable.

Yet even now, as though it were a thing quite separate from himself, his small body was pressing forward through the thick of the runners. His eye was caught by the flash of a red shirt that he knew must be from his own school. Slowly he was coming up to it. He made his way sideways between two larger boys and when another boy just ahead stumbled, sighing, and gave up John Sobieski dodged around him and into the free pocket, darting forward unhindered until he was running behind the familiar red shirt. When it found openings, he followed after. When it forced a way, shoving runners aside, he followed as though he had done it for himself.

They had passed over the parkway on a bridge of stone arches and were running on a bridle path that turned and climbed upward under trees around the bulk of a great hill. The stream of the pack had narrowed until it was only four or five runners wide, and at one edge the hillside fell away steeply — down to John Sobieski couldn't see what, though he was running on that side himself, just within the pack.

Twisting slowly uphill, flashing gay-colored, the pack surged over the crest and slid downward again, winding around, faster and faster. Somewhere John Sobieski had left the red shirt behind and now that the race was downhill he tried to break out and pass runners, but he couldn't, it was impossible with the runners pounding on all sides of him, he couldn't move from his place. He endured it until he couldn't any longer and then pulled abreast of the boy immediately in front of him and went through diagonally to the right. He saw he was free. He let himself out, his feet smashing into the ground in long downhill strides. But while he was passing exposed out there an impulse originating somewhere deep inside the pack reached him and struck him as the elbow of the boy beside him. For a moment he continued to run wildly along the edge of the hill, his arms waving and snatching for balance, but he was being toppled inexorably, and he went over.

John Sobieski went down running, but he

couldn't keep his feet. A young tree caught him by the arm, spun him around and threw him rolling down the slope. He hit things, but the pain wasn't as great as the exhaustion and sickness that came on immediately as he ceased running. He lay on dry leaves at the bottom, his body jackknifed and heaving. Overhead was the thunder of the pack, the rustle of feet among fallen leaves, the muffled reverberations of the shocks of a thousand galloping legs all shod in the sharp-pointed running shoes like hooves — passing by, pounding, and gone; a pause — a scattered hurry of stragglers, now one, now several, their breathing like the furious labor of bicycle pumps, their feet clumping — dying away; now all gone altogether — passed on.

    He was alone. Everything was quiet. A hot sickness, separate from the ache of lungs and throat went back and forth over him, for the first time unmixed with the bustle of others walking around feeling the same way. He hated his body that gasped and gasped for breath among the crisp leaves. He could not bear to think that even though he had lost he must still suffer for trying. For a while he didn't even try to get up. But he started to feel the cold on his arms and legs through his thin uniform. When finally he got to his feet he was so weak and listless he could hardly climb the steep bank. He pulled himself up from one tree to another, clinging to them on the uphill side, resting.

    Up on the bridle path again his coughing came over him. It began loud and wet and would get worse he knew, harsher and drier, but now it was all the same to him. He walked downhill weakly without purpose, staggering and coughing. As he came out of the woods the dark-haired runner, recovered from his run, his sweatsuit on, met him in the middle of the stone bridge over the parkway. Beneath them the bright automobiles whined in both directions. John Sobieski leaned on the boy and together they went down to the field, an enormous one big enough for twenty football games. On the far side the young coach's tiny car waited by itself and as they were crossing the man got out and came toward them.

"I fell over," John Sobieski tried to explain between fits of coughing. The man scowled, glanced briefly into the face of the other runner, and didn't answer.

They got him into his sweatclothes and inside the car. They rolled up the windows and laid him by himself on the back seat with the coats of the three boys thrown over him. The coach and the other two rode up front while John Sobieski coughed with a horrible crouping dry sound all the way back to their own city.

From where he lay he could see it growing dark outside. The shapes of roofs were sharp in the cold sky. He was aware of the fits and starts of the automobile and the traffic sounds of the city outside; of the rush of cold air entering and the voices of the two boys briefly saying good-bye; finally of the emptiness of the car with only himself and the coach remaining — when at last the car stopped for good.

John Sobieski Runs

"Is this where you live, John Sobieski?" the man asked from the sidewalk. He looked up at the gray two-family house while the boy climbed out past the front seat.

"Listen to me. You get into that house and don't come out of it for a month. You belong in bed, for God's sake. It isn't running anymore when you have to trade on your health to get a place. That doesn't do any good — it isn't reliable. Get in there and get better. Forget all about running for a while."

The coach spoke angrily. He held the car door open against the wind with his back and watched John Sobieski but the boy stood before him saying nothing. He got back into his car and drove away.

John Sobieski made his way upstairs. His mother saw at once that he was sick and looked after him.

He stayed in bed three weeks. Most of the time he slept. There was nothing he wanted to get up for. After the first week he didn't cough any more; as long as he didn't run it would be all right.

His father would come in to see him after supper. The older man seemed embarrassed. He would bring a kitchen chair and set it just inside the bedroom door and talk across the space at his son, who watched him from deep in the bed, his brown head against a big pillow.

"How do you feel tonight?"
"All right."
His father nodded. He wouldn't smoke in the

bedroom. He sat for a while. "I was in New York once," he said then. "I went on the train with my father. We stood up in some place and ate sauerkraut and frankfurts. That's all I remember about it." After some time he got up to go out. He stood with his hands on the back of his chair. "Rest up now," he said. "Stay where you are for a while. That's the only thing."

"Listen," John Sobieski said from the bed, "I'm going up there again once I get better."

His father looked down at the linoleum. His thick fingers lifted the chair and he carried it out.

In the darkened bedroom John Sobieski closed his eyes. He could hear the wind blowing outside between his house and the house next door. A boy moved before him in the dark; John Sobieski was coming up closer, from behind....He caught himself and swore and thrashed in the bed with regret. He couldn't remember his running without remembering his failure. Yet in twenty minutes more, going off to sleep, he would see before him a boy dressed in white pants and red shirt and he himself coming up behind, planning how he was going to take him.

The Proud Suitor

The Proud Suitor

About thirty years ago, when my father and mother were about to marry, there was a girl on our street named Marie Pulaski. She lived downstairs in the yellow house on the corner that they have just done over and are letting out in apartments to young married couples. My mother lived next door to where we live now, so she was just across, and down one, from Marie.

But my mother and her set were a lot wilder than Marie ever was. Evenings in the spring and summer when people used to sit out on their porches, and still do, for that matter, my father would come roaring and crashing and banging up the street in somebody else's automobile that he had managed to get hold of, and skip up the steps, dressed all flashy, to take my mother by her two hands and begin dragging her down from the porch; while she swore she wouldn't go anywhere with him or even get into his car, it didn't look safe. But he always managed to get her in there, even if

The Proud Suitor

he had to lift her up and throw her in, while the galleries on the porches, including Marie across the way, took it in; then they would tear off making all kinds of noise, with an old-fashioned horn blaring "Ska-googah!" because I guess my father couldn't ever borrow a fairly new automobile even in those days.

Nothing of the kind was ever seen to happen to Marie. She was a full woman already, being about twenty-four, with long dark hair which as often as not she wore in braids. She would sit out in the only chair on her porch, a rocking chair, and watch the tussles between my mother and father, and anything else that might offer in the street. She used to watch such things closely enough, though they never seemed to amuse her or make her indignant or anything else either. Her mother and father were quite old people who never showed themselves on the porch. As far as anybody could tell Marie never came out of the house at all, except to walk up the street to go to the store for her mother.

One night in the spring of that year, as people sat out on their porches after supper, something very funny happened. No sooner had my father clattered away with my mother beside him than queer, high-pitched cries began to be heard from down at the other end of the street. Then a man in a white shirt, with necktie flying and his black trousers flashing in long, strong strides, came running straight up the middle of the road between the houses; and as he came he shouted in a frantic, bushy-black-haired way, about every fifth step, "Stop! Stop! Stop!" But upon this final cry his voice seemed to give way, he himself collapsing along with it, for he pulled up and stumbled with a short little turn over to the curb. There he dropped down, his black-trousered knees knobbing high and his bushy head down between them, sobbing and moaning for breath.

But soon it was clear he was really crying, with actual grief, blubbering out loud on the curb over there across from our house. It seems the car my father had come to fetch my mother in that night was his; and not only that but he had only bought it two days ago — not that it was really a new car. He had been drinking beer in the grill down on the far corner, where my father used to stop in on his way up our street; and when my father came in and some of my father's pals introduced him as a man who had just bought a car, my father slapped him on the back in a friendly way and said that was fine, and he thought he wouldn't mind borrowing her for the night. The young Italian — he wasn't perhaps sure of the language yet but he was glad to be making friends — smiled broadly and happily. My father asked him to point out the car. He did. And with that my father, pulling out his watch first to make sure he was on time, jumped in and drove her off. The black-haired young man's smile left him slowly as he pondered what was happening. Then after a minute he sprinted up our street shouting in that way, and only gave up when he saw that his car had already turned the next corner and he found he just couldn't yell or run any more.

The people sitting out on the porches all knew my father pretty well, so they didn't have much trouble putting together what was going on. It must have been funny to them, to see that fellow out on the curb crying for all the world as though the car had been taken away from him, stolen, for good. But as they sat taking it in, waiting to see what he would do, somebody said, "Don't cry."

The words were out and hanging in the street between the houses, belonging to nobody, with nobody knowing where they had come from.

"Don't cry!"

This time the people sitting just across from the man made certain of something they couldn't quite believe at first: Marie Pulaski, watching everything closely as always, had not stood up but was leaning forward in her rocking chair and urging, positively ordering the young man not to cry.

But nobody, not even his mother come all the way over from old Europe, could have got through to him then. He sat on the curb and cried, and when he had got back his wind he picked himself up and walked down the street in the direction he had come, on the sidewalk this time, hanging his head and still crying to himself.

After the young man disappeared things on our street went back to what they had been before my father got there: the people sitting on their porches looking out. Marie sat on as though she hadn't done anything.

About dark, however, two men came walking

up the street and one was the dark-haired young man. They stopped over on the opposite sidewalk and the other, the taller one, pointed across at the house next door to ours, where my mother lived. Probably he was explaining that if the young man would keep in sight of this house he would be sure to see his car again before the night was over. Then the taller man went off on his own business, leaving the Italian standing there boldly with his arms at his sides, confronting my mother's house.

He stood there in this funny way until people were tired of watching him. Then, as it had been with the two words thrown out into the street a little while earlier, something happened — the man was all of a sudden gone — without anybody seeing just how it had come about. When after a little the streetlights had quietly come on and arranged in an instant the lights and darks of our street, he was discovered in a new place: sitting with his knees up in front of him again and his feet on the top step over on Marie's stoop, still watching my mother's house.

He had bought himself a good car, my mother says. They had gone all the way to the Adirondacks with it. They didn't get back until the wee hours of the morning, when they came tinkering up the quiet street and stopped. But before my father could turn off the ignition the black-haired Italian loomed up in the road in front of the car. My mother couldn't tell where he had come from, of course, and it frightened her.

"You come down," he ordered my father.

My father tried to kid around and carry it off, but the young man wouldn't have it. My father must get out of his car right away. It was a difficult situation for my father, with my mother up beside him. But he went around to help her get out. He didn't know if he was going to have a fight or what.

But my mother, with her boyish bob and all, had got over her fright and was taking it all in. And she says what she noticed most of all was that the Italian boy wouldn't look at *her*. It wasn't that he didn't want to, perhaps; but he kept his face turned away as if he was ashamed to have her see him. Even after my father had told her all about it later, as a joke, she still couldn't see the young Italian, as he stepped in front of the headlights and ordered my father out, as a fool worrying that somebody had run off with his new car. The car had something more to do with him somehow — she even thought it had something to do with herself. Not that the Italian had ever laid eyes on her before. But my father had taken his car and used it perhaps in the way it was meant to be used (my father is always using other people's things, which he says if they can't use them as well as he can they haven't any right to anyway) so that the Italian, whose car it really was, was seen to be without it in the eyes of my mother, while my father, who never had a car of his own, had made such use of it; and as a result the young man was ashamed. She was certain he would never forgive my father. Much my father cared.

The Proud Suitor

A few days later he showed himself again on our street. People might have expected he would come barging up in his own automobile, if he was going to come back at all; but no, he came on foot again, walking on the opposite sidewalk, about an hour after supper. It turned out he had sold the car already, after owning it just a week. He climbed up onto Marie's porch and spent the whole evening sitting on the stoop, for there was still only the one rocking chair over there.

The young man's name appeared on the wedding invitations at the end of the summer. They were from Mr. and Mrs. Wladislaw Pulaski and they requested the honor of your presence at the wedding of their daughter, Marie, to Mr. Giuseppe Verdi Abruzzi, of Italy, and for some reason one of them was sent to my mother. She was surprised. My mother being what she was, she had never had anything to do with Marie, and besides she was six years younger. But Polish weddings are something even now; what must they have been thirty years ago! My mother wouldn't have refused for anything.

So on the day of the wedding she had my father borrow a car and drive her over to the hall that Marie's father had hired for the afternoon. She arrived a little late. By that time the place was a regular little Poland. They were dancing and drinking, the music was going, some were singing, and there were long tables with rich heavy foods that she didn't know the names of. Couples came polkaing furiously by her, again and again, part of a big whirling round of people all turning on a single axis but all the time doing little epicycle whirls of their own as they came. My mother had no sooner got up to the edge when she was sucked off into it, a great big fellow with a flat Polish face simply taking her and polkaing her off, stomping, without so much as a word. But I don't think there was ever a dance my mother couldn't do, so off she went with him, having a wonderful time right from the start.

Except for one or two people from our street that my mother recognized, the wedding guests were all relatives of Marie's. The bridegroom hadn't invited anybody. He had simply shown up for the whole thing, dressed properly, all by himself.

Not that it seemed to bother him. On the contrary, he shone. In a white coat, with his handsome head of black hair, he went about with a radiant, proud and gracious air, as was required of the most important man there. The polka my mother was doing ceased all at once. There was a minute while the musicians — a piano was up on the stage of the hall and a man had an accordion on his chest — were seen to drink from glasses on the piano. Then they began to play a waltz. A wide circle at the middle of the hall seemed to empty itself as a round, cleared bowl, with all the ladies and girls there making up the sides. Then the young Italian stepped out into the ring, smiling, and delicately began walking around its edge, nodding and smiling with approval at this girl and that one until finally he chose, turning and bringing his feet together, bowing his head slightly, though looking up at the girl from under black eyebrows with laughing eyes, offering his arms. The girl placing her own within them, he took on a serious look and began to dance.

And the way in which he danced was not at all the way they used to do it at Cain's Dance Castle or the Pine Lake Pavilion or Sherman's Rendezvous in the Adirondacks, where my mother was always going with my father. It was what my mother and her crowd would have called "ballroom dancing." Not that it was any slower than what they did to the quick jazzy music she and my father liked; but it was a long and moving, round and full kind of dancing, a regular old-country waltz. My mother was charmed; she loved to dance. She had worked herself up to the edge of the circle, so when her big Pole presented himself before her in the same formal way she accepted him at once and they swooped off together. Then there were only the two pairs of them, the young bridegroom and his lady and my mother and her Pole, turning and turning and turning around the floor, past the watching faces of all the young girls. Then others came sweeping out, and soon the couples were all whirling and gliding and threading among one another. But through them all gleamed unmistakably the white coat of the young Italian, dancing with confidence, never so much as grazing another, beaming and smiling and nodding to everyone in his happiness and self-assurance.

Marie danced too, with all the young men, but of course she had to wait for them to come to her, and so she didn't shine as her new husband did. And except for the first waltz, which my mother had missed, they paid very little attention to one another, busying themselves instead with all the other men or girls each perhaps might have married but had not and now forever would not.

After the waltz there was a long noisy time when some of the people sat down at tables and ate, and Marie's old father came around to see that everybody was eating and drinking enough, and finally the musicians played another polka. Then, as they began a waltz again, all the women and girls, my mother included, crowded up in a circle; the bridegroom came around, and by some chance — perhaps he had seen how she danced with the broad-shouldered Pole when only the four of them had been on the floor — he chose my mother. And he knew who she was, not perhaps as he bowed, offering himself; but before they had turned once around the circle he recognized her. It seems a woman can always tell how it is with a man, when all of a sudden what she does or may think of him begins to matter to him. Another couple moved onto the floor, and another; the serious air with which the bridegroom began each waltz fell away, he became very gay and lighthearted. And his gaiety didn't radiate out all around him on the dance floor as before but instead was all directed to my mother. As for her, she was only eighteen, and he couldn't have been more than twenty. The grace with which he waltzed her, the wonderful gallantry of him,

The Proud Suitor

the very way he held her arms and guided her, and all the strange, bold, old-fashioned tenderness toward her that he made her feel was in him — it all overcame her and made her really shy with him, though I know they considered her a "fast" girl in her own set. When the waltz was finished he didn't leave her but led her to a table and gave her some of the food and some wine to drink. Then he was off around the hall again, gracious and benevolent with everybody. But he returned to my mother and polkaed with her and danced the waltz that followed with her. All afternoon he continued with her, and something began to pass between them, though everything they said was just ordinary, and proper to the occasion. But as he saw how my mother was feeling he looked glad, as though he would say, Ah, you do like this! And my mother responding by looking somewhat shy, as she really felt, though happy and excited, he would go on proudly, I knew it would be so! — and of course this made him, at that moment, all the more attractive to my mother. But even so it wasn't enough for him, for as they were dancing he suddenly looked at her with such pleasure and pride and confidence that he was making her happy that she understood he was going a step further; and though neither one had mentioned the first time they had met, she knew it was about that. You see I'm not what I might have looked then! You see what I can be on my own ground!

But as they were moving around the hall so gracefully, my mother looking all around her with such pleasure, she saw my father, who had come to pick her up, standing all by himself against a far wall by the door. She felt a pang. And although, she knew, the bridegroom had seen him too, he would not relinquish her; the waltz had just begun. It wasn't that he wanted to show off in my father's face or anything like that. He saw right away what my mother was feeling with my father there, but he saw too how attractive he still was to her, and insisting on that, he looked at her as if to appeal, But do you see it wasn't impossible?

When the waltz was over he left her and went to Marie. It was just past four o'clock. Within a few minutes the bride and groom had left the reception, leaving the guests to carry on by themselves.

Riding back to her house with my father in his borrowed car, my mother felt sad. She felt more at home with my father, but still she was about as unhappy as she had ever been in her life. It was strange, too, because she had always been so lively. My father drove along, looking very glum. My mother thought about the young Italian: how he had been when she first saw him, how he had got rid of his car and made up to Marie Pulaski, and how now he was married to Marie. She knew — and of course it made her proud — that he would rather have had her, or a girl like her, than Marie. That was what the car was for. But even with the car he didn't know how to go about it; he couldn't ever learn what a man like my father was born with. My father made a fool of him. So he sold the car and married

Marie. So it wasn't possible, he couldn't ever have taken her off in his car; and she knew she had to have a man who could. Still she felt sad, as though she had missed something. But she hadn't. Or if she had, how could she not have missed it?

My father drove along, in a bad temper, beside her. After all, they were supposed to be engaged. During the summer they had thought they would get married. They had talked about it on the way home from dancing in the Adirondacks at the same time that the Italian was courting Marie Pulaski. But they hadn't decided when. As they rode back from the wedding together, both feeling miserable, they made up their minds once and for all. Two months later on a Saturday they were married themselves.

Marie had always stayed pretty close to home. The only time she surprised anybody on the street was the night she leaned forward on her porch and told the young Italian he wasn't to cry. When he showed up afterward and spent the summer evenings on her stoop and finally married her, nobody was surprised. That was the way a girl like Marie was going to be courted and married — if she were going to be courted and married at all. If my father, say, had come along some night to pull her down to his car and take her out someplace — *that* would have astonished people.

After her marriage Marie lived in the same house, in the same flat even, downstairs. Her father, who owned the house, had turned out the renters upstairs and moved up there with her mother. Marie herself appeared outside as little as before. The following year she had a baby.

But the flat was wonderfully changed for Marie by her new husband. In it she would move about slowly all day and think about him in the city, working against whatever might be out there. She would wait for him at night with a deep and clumsy happiness that made him laugh at her when he came home. It isn't any wonder people saw so little of her, because she had no desire to go out anywhere. Even her father and mother left them pretty much alone.

As for the Italian, he throve. He became known on our street, and liked — not personally, because almost nobody knew him to speak to, but everybody approved of him. Those who were up early would see him come out of the flat at six, wearing clean work clothes with big stiff gloves stuck jauntily in his back pocket, and walk briskly, smiling and delighted, down the street and away. He came back around five in the afternoon with his clothes dirty but still delighted. It was impossible not to take to him. "That little Mr. Abruzzi is always happy," the women declared. "He might have a dirty job, but he never gets down." Nobody knew exactly what he did for a living though it was understood he worked for the city.

Marie herself didn't have any clear idea what it was her husband went off to do each morning. She admired him in his clean work clothes and supposed whatever he did out there must befit him. He on his side kept such things to himself and brought home the city's paycheck twice a month.

Times changed. The country went into the depression. Marie's husband got paid less; they shifted him from job to job, but they never let him go. Then my own grandfather got sick and my mother and father, who had been living in another part of the city, moved into the house we're still in to be near him. My father lost a lot of jobs around then, but he always bounced back with another one. At that time I was a small baby. My mother was proud of me; she liked to wheel me up and down the street, just to show the old ladies who'd always shaken their heads and asked what would become of her.

Looking out her front windows on bright October afternoons Marie would see my mother emerge from our house across the way, cross the street with me in the carriage and then head down her own sidewalk in the sunshine — since our side is in shadow in the afternoon. One day she bundled up her own baby, a girl named Thomasina, and set out after my mother. As my mother was coming along Marie came out with a big high-wheeled black carriage and started down the porch steps, so clumsy and self-conscious and proud of her own baby that my mother was sure the carriage would get away from her, and she left me and ran up to help Marie down with it.

They admired each other's baby. They took to airing the babies at the same time every day. They seemed to get along very well.

"Why d' you keep yourself so cooped up?" my mother asked. Marie looked at my mother. "Cooped up?" — she wasn't cooped up; chickens are cooped up. "I mean, what d' you do with yourself?" said my mother. "How come we never see you in the A and P?"

Marie had her groceries brought to the house by a Polish grocer who knew her father. My mother put a stop to that. "Why — who d' you think you are, the Rockefellers?" And on Saturday afternoon she dragged Marie down to the A&P. They left their babies with my grandfather and grandmother next door.

They came back with two boxes of groceries on a wagon, my slight little mother pulling and larger, grim-looking Marie walking beside. They went into our flat and my mother gave Marie our telephone and made Marie call up her Polish grocer. Poor Marie held the receiver out an inch or two from her ear and talked into the speaker without listening; my mother could hear the man arguing. She went and got some tea ready, but by the time she came out from the kitchen Marie had already gone in a panic over to my grandmother, retrieved her baby and taken it into her own house. Then she came out again and gathered up her groceries and retreated back inside — leaving my mother's shopping and wagon out on the sidewalk.

Marie's husband came home gay and confident

The Proud Suitor 169

in spite of bad times. Marie was late. He came in smiling and hung around the kitchen watching her work. In her anxiety Marie bungled everything; she spilled things — she broke a dish. He watched her, smiling. She was clumsy. Slow Marie, who had never been anxious before in her life, must have hated it. He saw the groceries — why were they different? Marie said nothing. He sat and wondered. Why were they different? Marie couldn't answer. Her head was all hot inside, her brain was smarting, she couldn't seem to say anything. The Italian looked at her, baffled, and went away. If only he had said something harsh, or even hit her as her father might have done, he might have made Marie happy again. But he left her anxious.

  In the evening he was troubled and uneasy until finally she was able to tell him how she had gone to the A&P with "the lady across the street." The Italian frowned. He knew my mother and father had moved in over there.

  I think probably Marie promised herself she wouldn't ever see my mother again. But Tuesday was bright and sunny after rain all day Sunday and Monday. In the morning her husband seemed cheerful once more, and in the afternoon my mother came out with the carriage and wheeled me down the street in it. Marie watched from her front windows and then looked around at her flat. After two anxious days she was glad to leave it. In a few minutes she was out in the street pushing her baby after my mother.

At the end of the week the house was again stocked from the A&P. We aren't Rockefellers, Marie repeated to herself; she wouldn't have called her grocer for anything. There was a general uneasiness in the house. Marie told herself she would find another grocer to deliver. But what she felt on seeing her husband, whose joy and pride in himself she loved, moving about uncomfortably and what she felt when he was away and she saw my mother out with me on the sunny street were two different things. And then she was such a placid person, she resented being troubled.

They were into November. The afternoons were cold. Marie took to having tea with my mother at the end of their walk. She would sit and listen while my mother talked on, and then all at once she would gather up her child and rush back across the street to start supper. My father was a salesman at that time, and sometimes when he couldn't sell anything he just came on home and forgot about it. Then all three would have tea over here and my father, all wound up with being home where it was warm and not out trying to sell things, would tease quiet Marie and call her "honey." Marie said "Mister" to him. "Aw, call me Jake, honey," my father would say. Marie would get flustered — my mother had to put a stop to it.

But our kitchen was so lively; on those cold afternoons Marie hated always to be watching the clock and then having to pick up Thomasina and run across the street. Her flat was dark when she got into it; she had a funny feeling of bringing in something that didn't belong there. One night in particular when she couldn't get rid of the feeling, sure enough her husband put down the paper he was reading after supper and sniffed. He stood up and walked around on the rug with a funny, serious look on his face. He came and stood over Marie.

"You smoke?" he asked, sniffing.

Marie couldn't even seem to say no. But when he had gone back to his chair she lowered her head and smelled herself. Cigarette smoke was on her dress, on her skin, it was in her hair; she was all covered with smoke she had carried in from my mother's kitchen. She went into the baby's room and smoke was on the baby, too.

Then at last one day Marie didn't make it back across the street in time, and when she came in her husband was sitting in the dark in his work clothes, thinking. And another day, a Saturday, as Marie and my mother came pulling their wagon together up our street, silly and having a good time, my father came out of our house for some reason and called down to them, and Marie cried out, "Hi, Jake!" and just at that moment her own husband, the young Italian, came walking the other way home from work, much more briskly than the two of them could pull the wagon in the silly mood they were in. He looked once across at my father and then went into the house without looking at the women.

"Must be afraid of us!" giggled my mother. Marie laughed, too.

The Proud Suitor

Marie admired my mother, who would chatter on, and smoke, and who always seemed ready for anything. But her admiration wasn't really anything until one afternoon, bundling up her baby, she heard an automobile horn in the street. She went out onto the porch. Standing at the curb was a little black Model A Ford coupe with my mother, one elbow out the window, at the wheel.

"What's the matter with you — you deaf? Drop Tommy at my mother's and hop in. Let's go for a ride!"

My father's company had given him a car to drive on his sales route. Marie hurried over to my grandmother with her Thomasina. "Let's try her out!" said my mother, and off they clattered down the street, the two of them in behind the windshield, Marie sitting high on her seat in the corner, grasping the door handle.

"Don't do that, Marie — you'll fall out. Light me a cigarette, that'll give you something to do. Where'd you like to go?"

And after a while Marie, seeing that my mother could make the car behave as satisfactorily as any other car they saw and smoke a cigarette at the same time, looked eagerly out at the houses and people they passed. They drove around town. It was a gray, cold day. My mother had to throw out her cigarette and put up the window. "Come on — where shall we go?" she asked Marie. Both women were excited. They wanted somebody to see them. "Listen," said my mother, "where's your Joe today? Let's drive over there and see him work

— see what they do when they get out of our sight."

Ordinarily Marie wouldn't have had the faintest idea where to find her husband working; but it happened that during the week a little older man called 'Fonzo had come to the house after supper to tell her husband something about Myron Street for the next day. It surprised her that she listened, but she made out, without thinking much about it, that they would be on Myron Street for some time.

Myron Street is just another ordinary street like our own, lined with two-family houses, only longer. The pair of women drove down it slowly in the little coupe without quite knowing what they were looking for. They came to a city truck with tools and cable on it, a yellow Men Working sign, some tools on the curb, red flags here and there and a few men standing around. It was late in the afternoon and bitter cold on Myron Street, with the wind coming steadily through. The men were filthy dirty, with their backs turned to the wind. My mother was for going over and asking for Mr. Abruzzi but the men just looked so cold, in a kind of angry mood from the cold, that she didn't. Heavy manhole covers were off all along the street. Men were in the holes, down out of sight. Squatting near the first hole was a man with a hard red face and red hands, who every now and then passed down a wooden piece three to four feet long with couplings at each end. The women went over and peered down the hole; the interior sides seemed made of muddy stones or bricks, and down in there a man, one knee in the wet bottom, was pushing the wooden rods one at a time into a narrow tunnel, just about big enough for a rat to crawl through, which seemed to run underneath the street to the next hole. The man grunted as he poked, his breath came up inside the hole and was swept away at the top, and once he picked up a hammer and swore and pounded at the rod when it stuck. He wasn't Marie's husband.

Down the third hole the young Italian was out of the wind at least, lying on his back with one of his arms entirely out of sight up the tunnel to receive the rods when they came through. To get into this position he must have had to squat down in the mucky bottom, drop onto his side in a ball with his legs tucked up, and then roll over on his back to extend his legs up the wet stone sides of the hole. His heavy work shoes, resting on the side of the heel, slipped around. He was feeling the same exasperated anger as the rest of the crew. He didn't mind working hard in the cold, with a chance to get it over with soon by steady work; but the sweat of morning, when work was exhilarating, freezing in its dampness at the end of the day he endured no better than anyone else. And as he had swung himself inside the hole this one last time, the asphalt of the road had barked his hand and broken the cold stiff skin and the hand had begun to bleed; but he got down anyway and reached up the tunnel, grappling for the rods — which would not come. He could reach in no further. His body wriggled as he tried.

The hole rose over him cold and wet, with a gray sky on top. Somebody was standing there looking in. It exasperated him the more. They wanted the rods before they even got them to him. He braced and wriggled and rolled on his bad hand; but helplessly — no rods were coming.

My mother and Marie — it was they who had appeared up above and not the man to receive the rods — stood looking down at him in the hole. He was wriggling and squirming on his back. My mother says he just looked "so comical" in there — his clopping big shoes rolling around the greasy sides of the hole with no place to grab! — that the two of them had to laugh, she bursting out first and Marie following after, and they stood there above the hole laughing; and at the same time they could see his effort — how hard he was trying at something and not succeeding; and they stopped. They just stood together. Then his wriggling subsided, and as he rested he looked up at them with exasperated, fatigued eyes and his mouth loosely open, breathing hard. He saw them. He stared up at them.

And they gazed down on him, in the hole. He writhed furiously a moment; he looked as though he wanted to catapult himself up out of there at a leap. But he was caught fast, with his arm in the little tunnel right to the armpit. As they stared down at him, fascinated somehow and without knowing what to say, he writhed once more, his big shoes slipped around and a knee came down and punched his face. My mother gave one laugh, like a high bark, in the wind. The man subsided altogether. He looked away and lay still, his eyes averted.

"Hey!" called my mother brightly, finding her tongue.

Marie knelt down in the road and bent over the manhole. But he would take no notice of them. "Oh, for cripes sake," said my mother. The man lay with an arm missing up the tunnel, his eyes open but turned away.

"Hey, you! What's the matter with you?" cried my mother angrily. Marie seemed to forget all about my mother. She leaned over the hole and said into it, "Don't cry. Don't cry." But her husband only lay there, and she started to cry herself.

My mother, running out of patience with the two of them, yanked Marie up from where she was kneeling and bustled her back to the car. She brought her back to our street and put her inside her house and left her there.

When after five days Marie hadn't appeared out of doors, my mother went over to see what was going on. The Italian hadn't been home since they'd left him. "He can't do that!" said my mother. She called up the hospital and the city and the police department. Marie wouldn't do anything. She wouldn't come out of her house. Then one day a little after Christmas a detective friend of my father's called up and said to my mother, "Say, Belle, you know that fella you was asking for? Well, he got a passport from the Italian consul around the first of December — in New York City." "God damn him!" said my mother. "What did he have to do that for!" "I don't know," said our detective friend. "Maybe he likes this fella Mussolini."

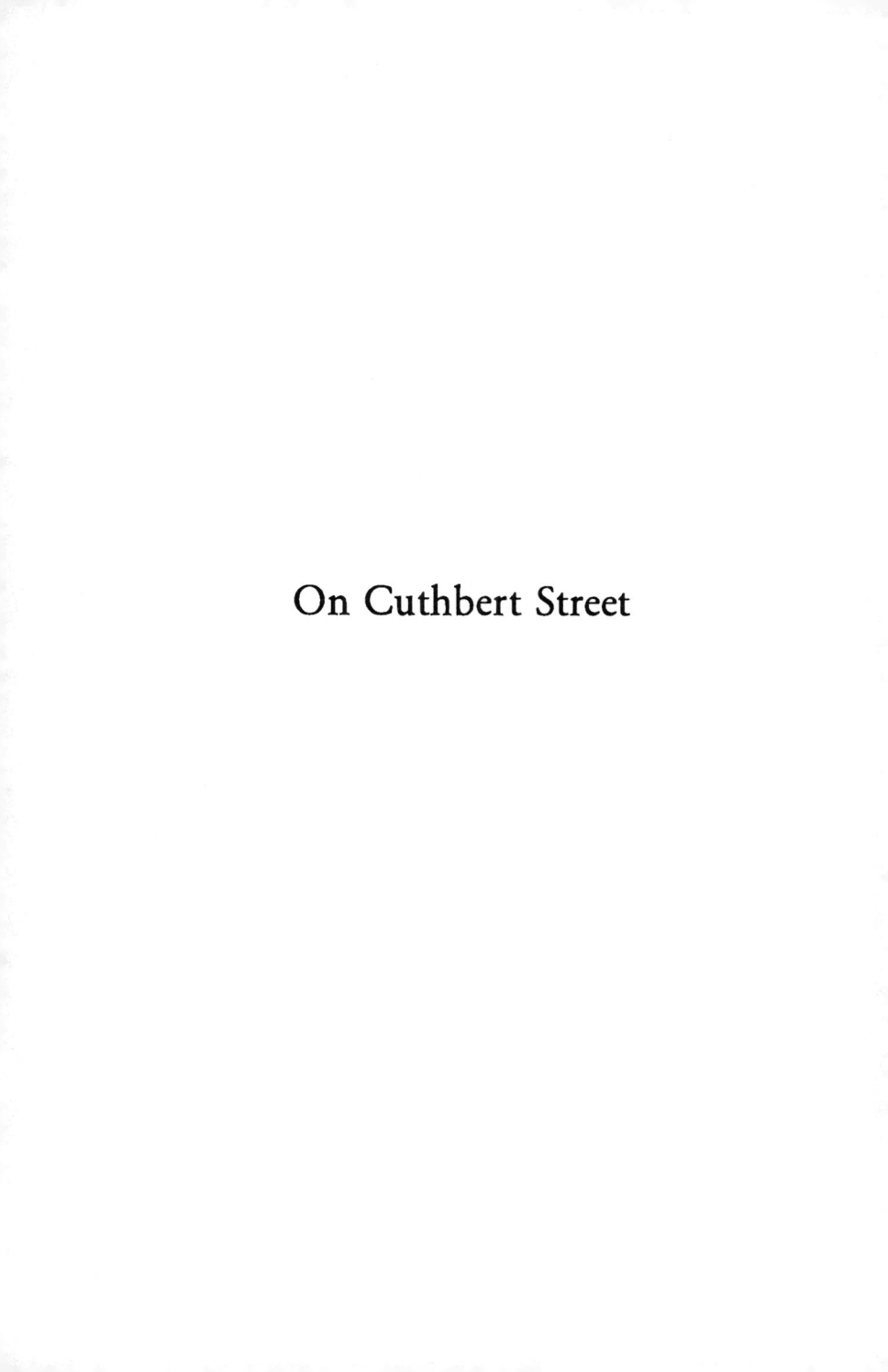

On Cuthbert Street

On Cuthbert Street

There was a momentary stir on Cuthbert Street years ago, when Lynne Bauer changed her name from Gussie.

You have to imagine Cuthbert Street as we who grew up there knew it. For us it was the permanent landscape, a valley made by the faces of long wooden two-family houses drawn up in opposing lines, with twin chimneys saddling their steep slate roofs. Deep within those houses, behind blinds and curtains, back underneath porches upstairs and down, people dwelt as in caves. You knew who they were. They knew who you were. You didn't just change your name; it wasn't your property.

Lynne understood that, well enough. She never tried to make anyone on Cuthbert Street, or in the neighborhood for that matter, call her anything but Gussie. Of course Father Irish, our assistant pastor, had always called her Augusta. But when she was fifteen, and went for the first time to the public high school on the other side of the city, she told all those new and strange people over there that her name was Lynne.

To those who had traveled with her on the bus from our neighborhood that morning the surprise was not pleasant. Arriving, they found themselves scattered among strangers in an enormous alien place. They felt confused and at a disadvantage. Only a few of them, it was true, heard her firmly contradict the new teachers who throughout the day called her name as Augusta, and these were in no mind to challenge one of their own. But they resented with a hot resentment. Who was she, to take advantage while they were feeling intimidated? Who was she, to behave so out of the character they had conceived for her? The girl was trying to put something over; worse, she was getting away with it. The new teachers understood nothing. The young but severe-looking Miss Meader, who used no makeup and wore round eyeglasses in wire rims, her hair in a bun like somebody's grandmother, even asked, with astonishing friendliness, how she spelled it.

"With two n's and an e," Gussie answered promptly.

"Two times the quantity n." Miss Meader, who taught geometry, changed the name in her record book.

"Plus e," added Gussie.

The teacher looked up. "You will be good at mathematics." She smiled.

Well everybody on Cuthbert Street knew that Gussie was smart in school — pretty smart anyway, if

On Cuthbert Street 183

not as smart as Richard Flaherty, who was supposed to have read the encyclopedia through already and played the violin, and developed photographs in his cellar laboratory. But Richard was a genius. If the teacher knew so much, why didn't she know Gussie's name.

But in the days and weeks that followed it appeared that nobody at the high school, except our group from Cuthbert Street — and only the girls really cared — knew Gussie's name. When you said "Gussie" over there, or even "Augusta'" they did not know who you were talking about and you had to say "Lynne" whether you liked it or not. Things were not arranged in this world as by rights they ought to be — which is to say, the way they had always been on Cuthbert Street. In the neighborhood they Gussied the girl relentlessly. But as she had always been Gussie with us, nobody paid any attention, except perhaps Father Irish, who didn't miss much. To make matters worse, as the year wore on they watched her form a new circle of friends, including especially the teacher Miss Meader. She wrote articles for the high school newspaper and signed them with her new name; she took a small part in a play, and her name was printed in the program. So they saw and heard more of it than was good for them. They saw themselves stranded, through no fault of their own, while she, who was no better than they were, they knew who she was, was carried farther and farther away from them on the stream of active life.

In one of these girls the bitterness of feeling

was lasting. Gloria Cherubini had been best friends with Lynne from the third grade through junior high school. On Cuthbert Street Gloria had always been the popular one — had been chosen class president year after year, and was the first girl their age to be asked out by boys. She was a tall, well-developed girl while Lynne was small, and known only for her friendship with Gloria. Now though, at the new school, it was Gloria who found herself sticking close to Lynne, as though for protection. In the thronging corridors Lynne darted ahead and Gloria was in a panic lest she lose sight of her. She would pull the smaller girl into a lavatory just for relief. At lunch, in the vast cafeteria, fifteen hundred people milled about and ate and talked at the same time. Lynne had established herself at a table and her new friends were attracted to it. Gloria usually got there first. She would watch them come up, their sharp eyes scanning the huge room with that look on their faces that said, "Where are the important people? There's nobody here!" Then they would ask in loud voices, "Is this Lynne's table?" Gloria, in a kind of panic, nodded and lowered her eyes and opened her lunch bag. Sometimes Lynne did not show up at all because meetings were held during lunch, and then Gloria felt herself isolated among all these loud, eagerly talking girls. More and more she rode back to Cuthbert Street alone, while Lynne remained at the school. They began to wrangle. Gloria accused Lynne of "leaving me alone" or "not telling me you weren't coming to lunch." Nothing Lynne could say seemed to do any good. Finally, in June, the friendship ended. "I don't know what to say to you, you're so unreasonable," cried Lynne in exasperation. "What should I do, to make things the way they used to be between us?" Gloria's face lighted up queerly. "Things won't ever be the same," she said with a perverse kind of triumph, "until you change your name back to Gussie."

But that wasn't going to happen and Gloria knew it. And maybe it was for that reason that, as soon as school was out, she went for a visit to her aunt's in Florida.

Down there she got in with a wild crowd. Her aunt was connected with racetrack people, and she brought Gloria back in time for the August meeting at Saratoga. They didn't come back to Cuthbert Street but stayed in a hotel at Saratoga, where they went to the races every day. Early one morning though, some girls met Gloria on the sidewalk outside her mother's house. Gloria's mother wasn't married to Gloria's father.

Gloria seemed to be waiting, so the girls stood with her. Then a car came along, a blue convertible they said later, with the top down. The young man driving had a deep tan; he wore a light-colored suit with very wide shoulders and long rolling lapels, and a soft white necktie arranged in a large Windsor knot. He might have been seventeen, or he might have been twenty-seven. Gloria got in next to him and the girls watched the car, with its Florida license plate, move swiftly away.

Gloria did not come home at the end of August.

She did not appear on the bus to the high school the week after Labor Day. In fact she was not seen on Cuthbert Street at all until that crisp blue Saturday morning in the middle of October when she emerged from our church, holding the arm of the darkly burned young man. Father Irish had just married them. Gloria made a tall bride, dressed in a well-cut traveling suit rather than a wedding dress. It wasn't a large wedding; only the half-dozen cars parked outside the church indicated that some such thing might be happening within.

The reception was upstairs in Gloria's mother's house. Lynne and two other Cuthbert Street girls had been invited. They were curious, and excited to be there. But they found Gloria inaccessible; she had removed herself at a stroke from them and their concerns. She behaved with such self-possession that they could only think of her as older and even, oddly, as something of a visitor. Her husband's name was Carmen. To these girls, Carmen and his friends were somehow formidable. They loomed large in their wide suits and were not at all like the Cuthbert Street boys on the school bus.

The gaiety was determined but brief. Father Irish made an appearance and drank a glass of wine with Gloria's aunt. Everybody knew that he went to the Saratoga races himself every year, wearing a short-sleeve white shirt and a jaunty straw boater. On this occasion, though, he wore his collar and cassock. He took the young man Carmen into a corner, where they were seen to speak seriously together and then shake hands. Shortly

On Cuthbert Street

afterward the whole party — Gloria's aunt, Gloria, Carmen, his friends, Gloria's mother and her husband — left for Florida. The flat would be empty, nobody at home there, for the next three weeks.

The three sixteen-year-old girls prolonged their walk home. Under the guise of walking each other to their houses they circled and criss-crossed the neighborhood many times. It seemed such a fearful thing to them; they all felt themselves vaguely on Gloria's side — left, somehow, with the obligation to defend her memory. Even more than the others, Lynne wished to stand up for her old friend.

"It isn't as if we never heard of such things," she said.

"Father Irish acted awfully normal about it."

"What was he supposed to do? Make them say they're sorry? Make them promise they wouldn't do it again?"

The three girls giggled hysterically. They had their arms around each other's waists and they wobbled for a moment, stretched across the sidewalk. Lynne, in the middle, hung on to the girl on either side. They were bigger girls in size and seemed more substantial than she felt, herself.

"When I think of something like that," she said seriously (Cuthbert Street never used the word love), "I think of somewhere else — somewhere far away, and someone I don't know yet. I never think of Cuthbert Street."

"Why? What's the matter with Cuthbert Street? These are awfully good houses. They don't make them like this any more."

The girls looked up and around. The ranked gables, the high slate roofs, made a jagged horizon against the blue October sky.

"I only mean, maybe she did the right thing — going to Florida."

"She won't be coming back to Cuthbert Street anyhow."

Small between the two larger girls, Lynne had a sudden sense of finality.

She asked her mother what she thought about Gloria's marriage.

Maxine Bauer, who was small and wiry like her daughter, shrugged. She had a way of wiping her face clear of expression, like a window with the shade pulled down. Her motto was, "The less said, the better done," and she used it now.

The girl smiled faintly. Her mother tended to say the same things over and over, for example, "Say nothing. Expect little." When, years before, the wide-eyed Gussie had answered, "No, I expect a lot," her mother had simply made her face smooth. When her husband, with a good job at the G.E. works, had died during the war she had gone down to the G.E. herself, saying only, "It isn't as though we never worked in our life before."

As soon as there were lights again where Gloria's mother lived (and at first you saw only a yellow square by looking down the alleyway between houses, nothing in the front rooms) Maxine went over with a small wrapped present to be sent on to Gloria and a loaf of bread from the Jewish bakery for Gloria's mother and her husband. To Lynne it was like visiting someone who had just moved to Cuthbert Street from far away.

Gloria's mother met them with a hard look. "It's all bungalows down there," she said, on a note of challenge. "They have a house to themselves."

Maxine Bauer made her face perfectly smooth. "Different places, different houses."

"He travels around," said Gloria's mother.

"As long as you have your work."

It was the girls and Gloria all over again, Maxine taking Gloria's mother's side, Gloria's mother avoiding out of the reach of her sympathy. Lynne moved closer to her mother; she experienced a peculiar, not unpleasant gathering in her throat.

But just after this, as Christmas was coming on and people were getting out their winter coats, the high school issued grades for the first quarter. For the first time Lynne received an A in every subject, and her picture appeared in the morning newspaper. She stood, because of her size, at the center of the front rank of seven girls. Richard Flaherty was in the picture too, but the boys were ranged behind the girls and you hardly saw him because he had always been short for his age.

Cuthbert Street was sure it was Gussie, but the newspaper gave her name as Lynne; her mother was asked about it over and over again. "Oh Jesus, Mary and Joseph," she wailed, upstairs in the house. "Why does she start now with this foolishness. I'm ashamed to go out into the street." And she really did hurry along the sidewalk on her way to the store, or coming home from work in the afternoon, in a furtive way that gave the girl a pang to see.

"It isn't some disaster," she tried to argue. "I can still be Gussie in the house. So what, if they call me something different at school?"

They were in the kitchen doing dishes. Her mother didn't answer directly but spoke in the grammatical third person, vaguely upward, to the shelf above the kitchen sink, "They don't even know what to call her."

"That's ridiculous. People call me whatever they want."

But she was talking to her mother's back. "You might as well talk to that wall," she thought, using, in her exasperation, one of her mother's phrases. "All right," she said aloud, "it makes a difference. People laugh at you. Nobody has a name like Gussie anymore."

Momentarily there was a stillness in the house. For Maxine Bauer, like her daughter, had almost no repose. Wherever she was, was activity. Now though, the uneasy dishwater was not sloshing, the pots and frying pan were not grating against the enamel sink bottom, the clink of silverware and plates as these emerged, rinsed, on the drainboard had ceased altogether. The girl held her position just behind and to one side, like the altar boy when there has been an unexpected pause in the ritual. There was the slightest tremor in the small wiry back that the girl recognized was as close to crying as her tough little mother would ever come.

She hung up her dish towel, put on her winter coat and went downstairs. She had to think.

Night had come. Cuthbert Street was long. The sky was dark and windy. She walked down one sidewalk and back along the other, like Father Irish when he would read his office. Until lately she had enjoyed her life. She had had to "nerve herself up" (as her mother would say) to change her name but the effort, when it came, did not feel like effort. Instead everything had given way before her and she had felt herself strong, as against other people. It had been a pleasure even, to think they would not dare such a thing. But Gloria had frightened her. She understood there was no forgiveness there; things had happened that were past calling back. Now there was her mother. For a single wild moment, walking in the cold, she imagined the houses themselves passing a judgment on her: her head drooped and the high structures, sharp against the remote stars, appeared in a mad way to have drawn themselves up closer to the sidewalks, squaring their porches like sternly folded arms.

"Hey — wake up!" came, in her ear, a high boyish

voice. "You blind or something?"

It was Richard Flaherty. She had walked right into him. "I'm going out," he said, taking her arm with two mittened hands, steadying them both. "To the drug store. To get more ink. To finish my composition. Walk me, come on." He pushed her off lightly like a boat run onto shore, steering her toward Broadway, where the stores were.

He was a small and quiet boy. The visor of his winter cap, which he wore with earlaps down as though he were much younger, twisted round and his face pointed eagerly into her own. Richard had been something of a fat boy, and had stuttered. Even now he spoke in bursts, with intervals between, so that much of what he said appeared to be the result of laborious thought.

She discovered that Richard admired her for changing her name. Since then he had not called her by any name at all, but now he promised to call her Lynne. "I'll have to say Gussie in the house, though," he told her, so gravely, like a little old man, that she nearly laughed. "My mother would agree with your mother."

It helped to have Richard Flaherty's support, but she needed more than that. Miss Meader's influence, she knew, did not extend to Cuthbert Street. So she lay in wait for Father Irish.

Every afternoon now in the cold weather she saw him out walking, a tall wide figure in cassock and biretta, his black cape as thick as an overcoat, reading his breviary in the fading light. She fell in beside him.

"Father, my mother is praying for me and I don't want it. Could you make her stop?"

This was the time when Father Irish was at the height of his popularity, when our old pastor, Father Hessler, had grown so crusty he did nothing but say his masses and hear confessions; and even then so few people wanted to confess to him that he would leave the confessional early, while on Father Irish's side of the church the pews were filled with people waiting. It was Father Irish who ran the parish. He said two Sunday masses, preached sermons, officiated at weddings, funerals, novenas, Sunday evening Benediction and the Stations of the Cross. He trained the altar boys and rehearsed the choir. He was a man of about forty, stout and red-faced, with curly black hair edging to gray at the temples and lively, even sparkling gray eyes. He had a strong singing voice that he was vain of, and used to effect in his sermons. It was said he had trained for the stage or the opera and had only entered the priesthood after a late vocation. His detractors (even at this time he had them) criticized his dramatic style; but most people liked it, just as they liked his fast driving in his black car, and the way he left his black clothes behind him when he went to the Saratoga races.

"Mothers do pray for their children, Augusta," he said, looking down at the girl with eyes that wrinkled at the corners. "Why would you want her not to?" For ten minutes they walked together in front of the parish house.

So Lynne went to meet her mother coming home from work, and on Cuthbert Street they encountered Father Irish. The priest faced them, taking up the whole sidewalk.

"I see by the paper, Maxine," he said, "that Augusta has made a name for herself."

He opened his great black cape and took Lynne under it on one side; he took her mother under the other wing, and embraced them both. "That's wonderful." His jolly red face gleamed with good humor in the cold afternoon. Maxine looked up at him, perplexed. Father Irish winked and gave her shoulder a squeeze, and turned to Lynne. "Your father would be proud of you."

"Now, you're joining the choir," he told her. "I want you at rehearsal Monday night. You'll be just in time to sing midnight Mass." Father Irish turned again to her mother. "That's all right then, is it, Maxine?" he asked in his bluff way. Looking across, Lynne watched her mother make her face smooth.

"If you say so, Father."

Between themselves they did not speak again about the name. On Cuthbert Street you hardly heard Gussie at all, any more. Father Irish made a point of calling her Lynne. Rarely, he would revert to Augusta, but always on a rising note of humor that served to reinforce the understanding between them. Upstairs in the flat though she remained, for her mother, unalterably Gussie.

On Cuthbert Street

You have to say for Father Irish that he recognized talent when he saw it; he had to. People forget that his job really was theatrical in its way. Besides the productions for the great holidays, Christmas and Easter, there were the morning masses to provide for, every day of the year. It was unthinkable that Father Irish or Father Hessler should be without an altar boy or choir even though only a few elderly women, the oldest on Cuthbert Street, might be in the church. Toward the end of his life Father Hessler sang all his masses in black vestments. When, hunched over with age and shortsightedness, the old pastor raised his nasal singsong, it was always with perfect faith that a response would come from the choir — and thanks to Father Irish, it always did. The choir might be, so many times, a single sixteen-year-old girl summoned by the sexton breathless from climbing her hall staircase when the scheduled girls had failed to show up. But Lynne knew that the ritual, conducted in earliest morning by candlelight in a language she did not understand (at school she had elected French as "more modern" than Latin), somehow connecting the living and the dead (it was only here that she thought of her father), could not take place without her. By comparison with what had gone before, she found this new part easy to sustain.

Spring came, and then early summer. Along the street the screen doors made a fuzzy barrier. One afternoon Lynne heard, from within the flat where Richard Flaherty lived, the sound of a violin; she had never liked it and she didn't like it now. Richard had disappeared into the technical side of the high school so that she never saw him.

Toward the end of the summer Father Hessler died. An old story about him, of how he had once stood up to the hierarchy and refused to send a considerable sum of money out of the parish, now brought priests from all over the diocese to his funeral. They parked their cars up and down Cuthbert Street and on the streets around. Little altar boys earned handsome tips carrying their black bags, and their starched surplices aloft on wire hangers, to the vestries and the rectory. Father Irish had organized everything. The solemn high mass was celebrated by the auxiliary bishop, but Father Irish served as subdeacon and preached the eulogy. He compared Father Hessler to the man in the Gospels who prayed in secret, rather than ostentatiously like the Pharisees, and who was therefore justified. Father Hessler, it seemed, had had no relatives; afterward people came up to Father Irish as though he were next of kin. He was in his element, his white teeth gleaming, eyes wrinkling at the corners. When the other priests had gone away he was left, as seemed right, in possession of the parish. But not for long; within a month a new pastor arrived, a sharp-tongued opinionated man of fifty who had no experience of the theater. And it wasn't long before Father Irish was transferred to an obscure chaplaincy, nobody knew quite where, in Albany.

Lynne missed Father Irish as she had not missed Gloria; with him she had no sense of unfinished business. She continued to sing morning masses, she understood it was not disloyal, right up until leaving Cuthbert Street for the teachers' college at Albany. With her state scholarship, won by competitive examination, she could afford to live there rather than commute.

Away from home, it does not have to be far, California or Albany is all the same, you do not think much about your native place; your new life absorbs you. All the same Cuthbert Street was there in the background, it was a necessary element in the exhilaration, the heightened sense of possibility, the girl now experienced. She was only twenty miles and a couple of bus rides away but Lynne returned infrequently and when she did, it was as a traveler coming home from things home knows nothing of.

Cuthbert Street wasn't where she lived any more. She would ask, without much interest, how people were doing there. They told her that Richard Flaherty had followed his father into the apprentice program for draftsmen at the G.E. works. Richard still played the violin, and had kept his reputation for genius. Lynne herself was remembered, after a few years, only as the girl who had changed her name in Father Irish's time.

To her old mathematics teacher though, the trip to Albany was just a beginning, a brief stop on the way to New York, where she spent her own weekends and school vacations.

Christine Meader was not yet thirty; she had earned her master's degree from Columbia and was working toward a doctorate. Lynne had been her favorite pupil if not, she had to admit, her best at mathematics. Perhaps she saw something of herself in the small, determined girl from Cuthbert Street. In any case, she felt a keen personal disappointment to see Lynne go to a state teachers' college so close to home. She had urged upon Lynne a real university, in New York or Boston, but had run up against something baffling in the girl, something she might have understood better if she had lived on Cuthbert Street herself. At the high school graduation the young teacher actually apologized to Lynne's mother, "I'll always be sorry we didn't do more for Lynne." Maxine, on her side, made her face smooth; she took Miss Meader's slender fingers in her own strong hand, like the masculine partner in a dance figure, forbearing pressure. "You shouldn't worry. Our Gussie was always a hard one to do anything with."

Amused, Christine Meader had to agree. Still, she was determined to see that her old pupil got her due. Over the next few years, she would stop off at Albany before taking the train to New York. She took Lynne to dinner, to concerts, to films the girl would not have gone to otherwise. On her side Lynne admired Miss Meader, called her by her first name, and took pleasure in being improved. Less frequently, the girl might be persuaded to go to New York herself. After three years she could find her way around Grand Central station and Morningside Heights, but she felt that New York was not a place where she, herself, had any business just yet. Her college life was enough for the moment. She majored in mathematics; or rather, in the teaching of mathematics. Christine Meader approved the emphasis. "You have so much will," she said. "Mathematics doesn't really yield to that, but people do." And because Christine Meader recommended it she signed up, in her fourth year, for a class in English literature.

The class, which was part of the evening division, reminded her of Cuthbert Street. The lecture hall was old and too large; the dark wood of the desks was deeply scored, and you could see the night sky outside behind broad windowpanes. The students were people who had worked all day, gone home and changed their clothes, and then come out after hours with a look of putting their minds to serious things. The teacher was a neat white-haired man with a gentlemanly manner, named Ramsay; he wore small bow ties and had retired from Union College. He addressed them formally but did not lecture. Much of the time he simply read to them aloud.

One night he read "Lycidas."

When he had finished, at the end of the hour, and the students had gathered their things and left, in silence as though after a service, he saw quivering among the middle seats the squarish blocky white shirt and lowered head of the young man he knew as Arnold Fowler, who was trying to suppress his sobs. Professor Ramsay was gratified, but not surprised. From experience he knew that his evening students were closer to feeling than the professionals, as he called the daytime undergraduates. Still, "Lycidas" was a poem that even he felt to be artificial.

"Weep no more, woeful shepherd, weep no more," he quoted lightly, coming forward, "for Lycidas, your sorrow, is *not* dead...."

Smiling, the teacher turned for confirmation to the only other person remaining behind. "Actually he'll never die, will he, he lives in the poem."

Lynne had something of a rapt look about her, of having only just shaken herself awake. "It's like Latin, when you read," she said. "Even when I don't understand the words it doesn't seem to make any difference."

The young man, Arnold Fowler, recovered himself and stood up. He put on his coat and Professor Ramsay got them outside into the cold air, which roused them both. Once in a booth in the nearest grill, with glasses of beer in front of them, the three could laugh together over Lycidas.

Arnold sat by himself on one side of the booth. He had blond hair cut very short, a broad forehead and altogether a firm and rocklike appearance; but his eyes were troubled.

"I shouldn't have cried."

Lynne agreed with him. Even now she wasn't over the idea, deeply held on Cuthbert Street, that crying represents weakness or cowardice or both.

"Why, how could you help it," laughed Professor Ramsay, "when 'daffadillies fill their cups with tears'? What do you say, Miss Bauer?"

"I think it was sad. You *shouldn't* die, when you're so young."

She heard the vehemence in her own voice, and only then was she aware of feeling what she had said; for the first time she looked across into the young man's earnest, rueful face with some sympathy.

"You shouldn't, of course; not if you could help it."

Professor Ramsay placed a consoling hand on Arnold's overcoat sleeve. "You imagine how terrible it would be for yourself. That doesn't mean you are afraid; it only means you have so much you would regret. It's the feeling of the poem, Mr. Fowler."

Lynne felt a sudden warmth pass over her, and a not unfamiliar constriction in her throat. Arnold turned upon the girl the earnest eyes that made him resemble, looking directly at her, the posters of the Rev. Billy Graham.

"You're smart," he said, as he escorted her, walking properly on the outside, back to her dormitory. "Tell me whether I should have cried or not."

It was early spring, and cold. Arnold, bareheaded, was an erect and solid figure in the wind. He did not presume to take her arm. Lynne had to wrap her own hands around his sleeve, walking in the shelter of his coat. She reassured him.

Arnold was a test engineer at the General Electric. Over the next weeks he explained himself to the girl, and on weekends to her friend Christine Meader as well. He had been in the Army in Japan and then to R.P.I. on the G.I. Bill. On the front seat of his car he kept a little book, *Fundamentals of Servomechanisms*; he studied it everywhere, slowly, reading a page and then visibly thinking, as he sat in the glass corner made by his windshield and the rolled-up side window. "That's a very important book," he told the two women earnestly. Did they understand that in a few years the General Electric wouldn't have just a single home city, as it did now; that the company was going to set up smaller operations all around the country — all around the world, in fact? "A great chance, for an awful lot of people." Day or night, Arnold wore starched white shirts. He might loosen his necktie, but he never removed it entirely. "They say if you wear a blue shirt you'll be passed over for promotion," he told them, laughing. "I don't know if it's true, but why take the chance?"

Christine Meader approved of him. He came from a small place in New Hampshire, and his upbringing was old fashioned. He didn't smoke or swear; he opened doors and placed chairs for herself and for Lynne, and deferred to them with respectful seriousness. With her it was a recommendation, that he had cried over

Lycidas. In the end Lynne, too, liked him for this; it was so unlike what she had been used to on Cuthbert Street. As she knew him better she understood he was tough, and he worked as hard as she did herself.

They became a couple — at least in Albany. Cuthbert Street knew nothing of Arnold, and took notice of Lynne herself only once in her final year at college. On Good Friday she was seen in front of her mother's house, stepping from a black car driven by Father Irish. He had brought her home for Easter.

The motor never stopped running. Lynne walked around the car and hung for a moment over the driver's window. It was the time of day when, years before, Father Irish had prowled the sidewalks and now, as the car moved away slowly between the houses, there were people out; a woman in a white kerchief, carrying a black pocketbook, waved, and from behind his windshield Father Irish smiled and nodded acknowledgment. Cuthbert Street doesn't forget.

She had come across Father Irish again in front of the main bulletin board. She knew him at once, though something in the bend of his neck, as he leaned forward under the familiar cloth cape to read the notices, made her think rather of old Father Hessler. When he turned and recognized her his eyes lit up in the old way, his voice sang, "Augusta!" and he placed his hands on her small shoulders. He claimed her for the Newman Club he had been directed to organize at the college.

Lynne brought her friends into the Newman

Club with her. It surprised her that Father Irish scarcely held meetings. Instead he would show up at ten o'clock at night to call a study break and take half a dozen of them for a beer or a sandwich. He didn't seem like a priest at all, he was interested in their classes and seemed to know as much as their teachers. Once, when Arnold came along, they talked of poetry and Father Irish recited Shelley, "Hail to thee, blithe spirit!" for three verses, in his fine rich voice. Arnold's eyes shone.

"What do you think of Milton, Father? He made me cry."

"A genius and a heretic," replied Father Irish, but absently. He sat, suddenly abstracted, letting the talk swirl around him while he thought of something else.

But for all Father Irish didn't seem his old self, he didn't miss much. "This Arnold of yours," he said to Lynne as he drove her back to Cuthbert Street for Easter. "When are you bringing him around for instruction?" She laughed, and Father Irish laughed; she had known Arnold barely two months.

But Arnold was the reason, in June, that she stayed on in Albany after graduating. She took a job at Woolworth's and lived in a small room. Arnold arrived every night just after six, and they drove out. They drove in every direction — west beside the Mohawk River, that reflected the low sun, in the direction of Utica; north toward Lake George and the Adirondacks; south to Kingston, with New York at the highway's end; and on the weekends east, once with Christine Meader and after that without her, to Tanglewood. It was a courtship by automobile, a nightly rush through air and space outward, seeking the trajectory's outer limit, the exact point where gravity — the necessity of being at work in the morning — must assert itself; then would come the dark return plummet under white sparky stars and enormous standing black tree-presences. It excited them both, to try how far they might travel each night before turning back. In August they decided to marry, and she sent him to Father Irish.

"Why should I be doing this?" he asked cheerfully enough, from behind the steering wheel as he set off. Lynne was unable to answer.

Arnold returned to her with a furrow in his square forehead, as though he were trying to understand something in Professor Ramsay's class.

They sat in his car, now parked at the curb, talking. It was not that he would not take instruction, she saw; it was that he could not. "You know, my father belongs to the Salvation Army. So did my mother, while she was alive." He faced her with the same rueful look she remembered from their first meeting. Lynne realized it was for her to reassure him, and restore his temporarily disabled strength. "Look," he said to her finally, his eyes still troubled, "I'll go to New Hampshire and think it over. I'll talk to my dad. But I don't think I could do it."

Alone in her room, Lynne was dismayed. She

felt herself under some old Cuthbert Street burden. Nevertheless she determined that, if Arnold could not, then she herself would have to. Anybody might marry them, after all.

She saw him off late Friday afternoon. The next day, instead of talking to his father, he hiked up a mountain. The thermal winds built up a thunderstorm through the hot afternoon, and as Arnold left the tree line and came up onto the exposed summit a bolt struck the frame of his rucksack and knocked him flat. He was found by a party of hikers before nightfall and brought down. But before he reached the hospital his heart had stopped for good.

Of course people are killed every year by lightning, but Lynne went numb. She would not go outdoors. She could not bear the sky. She spent days in bed. She had confused dreams. Though she had never climbed mountains she imagined herself in them, great slabs of gray rock all tilted awry. You were not, as she had supposed, alone in them but on the contrary you were being watched. Something was watching you from beyond those those gray sharp edges.

Lynne came back to live on Cuthbert Street with her mother upstairs. At first she did not come out at all. By the end of January, though, she was well enough to take a job at the high school — the job Christine Meader was leaving in order to finish her Ph.D.

"It might be all right for a year or two." Miss Meader eyed her old pupil doubtfully. "But you don't want to go over your old tracks forever. Plan to come to New York."

Lynne found teaching hard. What it demanded, more than anything else, was nerve. And she felt herself flattened, without substance, as though she were the one who had been struck by lightning, and serve her right. She felt like an imposter, she dreaded going to the school each day. It was her mother who kept her up to it. "It isn't as though you were never there before. It can't be so different just because you're the teacher." Outside in the street when people asked, Maxine made her face smooth and told them, "Our Gussie always managed." Nobody denied that. Late in the winter as the G.E. reorganized and transferred work elsewhere, Maxine was laid off. Being the breadwinner settled Lynne somehow; her job, if hard, became manageable. "Just pay the bills, and things will be all right," she told herself. It was one of her mother's phrases.

She was advisor to the school newspaper. One night she worked through supper and then very late afterward, pasting up the dummy. She came home from the bus along the cold street past the two-family houses that were so high and so deep, fastened so securely against everything outside that no wolf's breath would ever blow them down.

"Wait a minute," came a voice from behind her. "I'll walk you."

Richard Flaherty came up alongside. Lynne was the same size she had been in high school; Richard himself had grown only a little taller, but his figure was somewhat thicker. The tilt of his face, under the fedora that he now wore like the men on Cuthbert Street, showed the same eagerness as he peered into her own. She understood that Richard's admiration was a permanent thing. "I'll come to your house," he said when he left her; and he did.

Maxine, who had never taken to Arnold, liked Richard well enough. Richard was tactful; he never called Lynne anything but "you" in front of her mother. When she realized this, she wanted to do something for him. As though she were Christine Meader now, and he were herself, she urged him to go away to college. But Richard knew better. "You can't get better training than I've had anywhere," he told her seriously. "College doesn't mean a thing at the G.E. Look at Vince Schaeffer. Never went to college. Never even finished high school." Vincent Schaeffer was the General Electric Co. scientist who had gone up in an airplane and dropped pellets of dry ice into a cloud to produce, for the first time, artificial snow. Cuthbert Street knew his name, while it did not know the Company's Nobel Prize winners, because he had grown up only three streets away.

When Lynne did leave the high school two years later it wasn't to follow Christine Meader to New York, but to marry Richard Flaherty. Father Irish returned to Cuthbert Street one last time to perform the ceremony,

On Cuthbert Street

for which he used her baptismal name, Augusta.

    The simplest thing seemed for Richard to move in upstairs with Lynne and her mother. Besides himself he brought his violin, his drafting tools, his encyclopedia and a few other books, and two cameras. The rest of his equipment he left in his laboratory in his father's basement.
    Lynne got pregnant right away. The doctor warned that delivery would have to be by Caesarian section. The operation was severe; during Lynne's recovery Maxine cared for both her and the baby. It was at this time that Richard borrowed some money from his father for a down payment on the house, and got started in his sideline of photographing weddings, graduations, and anniversaries. He was sincerely grateful to his mother-in-law. When he saw that his playing bothered her (or his wife or the baby, he couldn't really tell), he took the violin down the street to his laboratory. What with his violin, his photography, and the doctor's warning him severely that any further children his wife might have would be by Caesarian section also, that there "wasn't much left" for that and the best thing he could do would be "to leave her alone," Richard spent much of his time there, even after Lynne was well enough to return to school.
    He did leave her alone. Not that it was easy. Not that he said anything. He was too diffident and too

inarticulate for that. No, he simply looked to Lynne with a touching faith that somehow she would work things out.

Maxine, who had talked it all over with the doctor, was of two opinions. "He can just leave her alone," was one of them. On the other hand she didn't want to be unfair, and sometimes she thought, "He doesn't drink. A man has to have *some* fun."

Once again Lynne had to nerve herself up. She went to a new young doctor downtown, and of course she avoided the drug stores around the corner from Cuthbert Street. She brought the prescription home, removed it from its plain brown paper bag ("as if it were Kotex," she said to herself) and set it on the dining room table where her husband and her mother could see it. She left it out there for three full days.

Richard Flaherty was relieved. If you wanted to call it sin it was hers, not his, and that relieved him as much as anything. He knew himself. He was a good enough person, faithful, he played by the rules, but he couldn't have promised to stay away from her forever, and he admired her for cutting through a knot he could never have untied himself. But even he was surprised when, from this time, his mother-in-law began to call her daughter Lynne. It was, Richard reflected, remote in his cellar darkroom, a result comparable in its way to Vince Schaeffer's, when he first seeded the clouds with dry ice and made it snow.

Magister Pietro

Magister Pietro

Father Irish came to Cuthbert Street when our old pastor, Father Hessler, had already been a caretaker, more or less, for years. Nobody remembers the assistant before him.

He was a tall and heavy man with black hair and eyebrows, snapping blue eyes, and a rich baritone. We all understood, though we never heard it from Father Irish himself, that he had trained for the opera but had, instead, entered the seminary just as he was about to begin his professional life.

Father Irish revived the parish single-handed. Before long the congregation was coming willingly and in numbers not only to Sunday mass, but to a whole range of services besides: evening novenas, the forty hours' devotion, the Stations of the Cross during Lent, and even the drawn-out morning services in Easter week, as on Holy Thursday when the institution of the Eucharist is commemorated, and on Good Friday when no mass is said at all — the only day of the year when this is so.

Those who did not attend such services could be certain that, at any rate, they were taking place; and the knowledge gave a deep confidence that life was after all regular and secure, it was tolerable and might even be, in limited ways, happy.

The spectacle, the drama, of the altar was everything to Father Irish. He found a sexton to care for the sacred vessels, and women to look after the priests' vestments and the altar cloths. But he rehearsed the choir himself, on Monday nights; and on Tuesdays, after school, he trained a whole new corps of altar boys. We learned to say the Latin after him by rote, like a poem or song, before we ever saw it printed out or knew the meaning in English:

*Ad de-um qui lae-ti-fi-cat
ju-ven-tu-tem me-um*

All our movements, too, like the genuflection, or the simple and profound bows; our attitude, when standing or kneeling; our gestures; our handling of the missal, the bell, the cruets of wine and water, and so on — were learned by imitation. We mimicked Father Irish and Peter DiDonato, who was older than we were and the only holdover, in everything. It was like learning to dance, or to play music, or to wrestle. These things can be shown, but for the most part learning them happens without words. In the Uffizi Gallery, in Florence, there is a marble, dating to the third century, of two wrestlers:

the figure on the bottom is solidly based on his knees, toes curling forward like a sprinter's ready to spring; above him, the dominant figure has initiated a move that any wrestler alive would recognize as the Cross Body Ride. When you think that the marble is itself a copy of an earlier Greek bronze, you realize that the knowledge of this complicated move has been preserved through more than twenty centuries not by the sculpture that represents it (only accident has preserved the sculpture) but by direct and wordless transmission — living human beings observing and imitating others, practicing, becoming expert, themselves in turn becoming the objects of imitation — through all that time. So it was with us and the altar: we imitated and practiced, and took a profound satisfaction in doing the smallest things (as that the wrestler's toes must be turned forward, not backward, when on his knees on the mat) correctly. We were well taught, but quite differently than at school — there, it was all explanation, in writing or in talk; and if you could explain something, you were giving proof that you knew it.

There were, besides, the roles to consider.

Every Sunday night, at seven o'clock, there would be the Benediction of the Blessed Sacrament, with procession.

In the beginning, as a sort of outrider or precursor, would come the Thurifer, with the thurible hanging from several long chains gathered into his left hand, his right hand pressed against his surplice at his breast.

This boy would have to be short, or of middle height, so as not to detract from the Cross, which introduced the procession proper.

The heavy Cross, six feet high upon its shaft, had to be carried boldly, absolutely straight, with inexorable steadiness sweeping everything ahead of it. The crossbearer had to be tall and dignified, his expression grave and even solemn, to make clear that the procession coming after was one of the most serious affairs in life.

The two Acolytes, coming next, side by side, carried lighted candles in tall brass candleholders. Preferably these would be short boys. Then would come all the extras, hands clasped, expressions severely controlled (especially the eyes), ranged two and two, taller and taller back to the figure of Father Irish himself, dressed as though for a journey in the wide cream-colored cope with hood at the back, and wearing the black biretta that he wore even outdoors when reading his office on the sidewalk on Cuthbert Street. Just in front of the priest walked the most important of the altar boys, the Master, or as Father Irish liked to say, Magister.

The Master had to be an impressive figure. Size had something to do with it; but above all, the Master's demeanor and bearing had to reflect an awareness of the significance of his function, which was to assist closely and directly the priest, upon whom hands had been laid in the sacrament of Holy Orders. Father Irish was a large and heavy man and his Master had to be chosen accordingly.

In procession the Master carried the small gold boat filled with incense. Father Irish generally avoided having him walk beside another boy, even if they were of a size. He preferred his Magister alone. On occasion he might even walk the odd boy single, and himself together with the Magister make a final pairing of solemn and dignified figures.

A few minutes before the half hour we would gather by the sacristy door for Father Irish to choose the parts. He did it swiftly and surely, like any good coach. There was no bickering; if you wanted a part you asked for it beforehand and Father Irish considered it while he was vesting. Father Irish might joke quietly, perhaps, about "bearing your Cross." Once he said to Peter DiDonato, "Pietro — take up thy Cross, and go before me."

This, however, was really a very special occasion, when a preseminarian, an old friend of Father Irish from his last parish, was visiting and took the role of Master. This boy was tall and blond and, though thin to the point of being gaunt, very good-looking; he walked beside Father Irish as though he were a priest already, and some in the congregation even supposed that he was. Certainly there was between the two a connection subtle but unmistakable, and in the altar boys' vestry afterward we all agreed we'd never seen the part of Master played so well. Possibly Father Irish had had something like that in mind. At any rate, he invited Peter DiDonato to have coffee and dessert with him and the visitor afterward, in the parish house.

Peter DiDonato was our usual Master. He had been an altar boy for seven years and had become inseparable from the role. In his last year of high school he was tall, with Italian good looks, large expressive eyes and bright teeth, when he smiled, against his lean dark face with its well-defined aquiline nose. It was said, and it was probably true, that at one time or another every single one of the choir girls had had a crush on him.

Peter had always been Peter in the neighborhood — he only became Pete in his brief career as a high school football player. In tenth grade, though he had never played football before, he became a very good end on the varsity. But the next year he refused to go out for football at all, and the coach had to give up on him finally, saying, "It's no use expecting Pete to play ball, he doesn't think it's worth doing. He's thirty-five years old already."

The DiDonatos lived in a little bungalow on Cuthbert Street, three blocks from the church. The whole family was musical. Peter's beautiful older sister, Gemma, sang in the choir, his brother Al played the accordion, and his little brother, Eugene, carried a rounded suitcase in the shape of his French horn to school every day. Eugene was one year younger than I was. But in tenth grade he was as tall as Peter (Al, who was my own age, never did grow tall and never got beyond Thurifer) and already going down to Philadelphia, every other weekend, to study with the first horn at the Philadelphia

Symphony, and something of a wild man, besides. He let his hair bush out, he shuffled his feet and played rhythm on the desk tops at school and called everybody, even the teachers and girls, "man."

But the only reason to describe Eugene is to point out how different his older brother was. Even at school Peter had the sort of dignity he showed on the altar. The coach had been right, he was an adult at sixteen, and it was no surprise to anybody when he left off playing football. "When I became a man I put away childish things," said the sardonic teacher of American history, Mr. Marcel, when he heard of it. But even Mr. Marcel was unwilling, in the end, to challenge that dignity in the classroom. Once, after closing his *New York Times*, that he used as a shield against the noise as the students came into his class, and coming around to the front of his desk, carefully buttoning his double-breasted suit, he wrinkled his brow and screwed up his owl's eyes and then suddenly thrust out a long bony sardonic finger and demanded, with a thin smile, "What is money, Peter? How can the government say they're out of money? Why don't they just print it, if they need it?" Peter faced that finger, that voice, that sharp predator's eye with perfect composure — but remained silent. Peter's expression and bearing were respectful, but in them Mr. Marcel must have read somehow the message *Noli me tangere*, because he quickly shifted his attention to the girl sitting in front of Peter. Grace! What is money? Who paid for that dress you're wearing? Where did your father get the money? And where did the General Electric Company get it? Oh, your father got it from the bank! And where did the bank get it? And so on. Maybe Peter understood, about money, and maybe he did not; but it was hard, even for Mr. Marcel, to imagine taking him through the subject as Mr. Marcel took the flustered Grace. He certainly gave an impression of intelligence, of seriousness, of deference to his teachers ("For I also am a man subject to authority," quoted the sardonic Marcel); and so it was something of a puzzle why he did not do better at school. The football coach told his friend Marcel that he thought it was school itself, and not just football, that Peter found childish, but Mr. Marcel, who belonged to our parish and so had an advantage, only muttered, "Thou art Peter, and upon this Rock," and suggested, tartly, "that we return him to ecclesiastical jurisdiction."

Mr. Marcel was only expressing what the parish had felt for some time, that Peter DiDonato was destined for the seminary. It was what the part of Master, played long enough, led to. The altar boys all conceded the role and Father Irish, once he had filled the other parts with the talent available, always ended with the words, his eyes lighting up as they came, finally, to rest upon the tall, serious figure beside him, "....and Magister....Pietro."

My own role at this time (I was in the eleventh grade) was Thurifer. I took over the part from Peter's brother Al. We had always been about the same size. When younger we had often carried the candles in procession, and served our week of morning masses together. Father Irish assigned the two of us to old Father Hessler because we both said the responses so distinctly. Sometimes one of us might stay to help Father Irish vest and then, if necessary, to serve his mass as well.

As we both got older, new boys succeeded us as Acolytes. Then we tried out as Thurifer, Cross, and even, on occasion, Master. But neither of us had the build for Cross, and Master was out of the question.

So as the incense came more and more to me, Al dropped the altar, as we said then, and went up to the back of the church and sang tenor with the choir.

I say that the part came to me, more and more. I could have said that Father Irish chose me for it. The truth is, though, that I chose it for myself. I loved being on the altar. I liked the music, though I wasn't really musical as the DiDonatos were. I liked saying the Latin, moving the great heavy missal at mass, pouring the wine into the chalice and the water over the priest's fingers. It was all like a play, and I had this notion about it: I could never think of the church as having a ceiling — somehow it was, in my mind, roofed instead by the dark and jumbled sky, just breaking into light, that I would see in the early morning over Cuthbert Street on my way to serve. So for the evening novenas, or Sunday night Benediction, I would always walk through the streets early and then duck inside the altar boys' vestry and put on my cassock. Then I would light a candle, get ready the censer, take a charcoal cube in the tongs and blow the corners of it into orange sparks. The thing was to have a good glowing coal or two when the time came for the three of us — Father Irish and Peter DiDonato and I — to stand together at the foot of the altar; and I would raise the hot brass lid with the middle chain, at the same time swinging the lower pot, containing the radiant coal in its bed of ash, up to the level of their hands where Peter opened the incense boat and Father Irish deftly, in two nice gestures, spread incense grains over the fire; and the fragrance and smoke tangled in our nostrils and then rose into the upper shadows of the sanctuary and quickly spread throughout the church.

The censer wasn't easy to manage: it hung on three chains, and the lid had to be raised by means of a fourth chain at the center of these. It would be easy to tangle the chains, or spill the pot, coals and all. But I got to be very good at it. I liked leading the procession, forerunner even to the Cross. But my great moment came when the priest, with the Blessed Sacrament in the monstrance, turned (Father Irish always turned with a certain abruptness so that the movement, though expected, caught us all ever so slightly by surprise, as, perhaps, the Transfiguration caught the two apostles by surprise) holding the sacred instrument in the folds of his cope and the humeral veil, which Peter DiDonato had laid across his shoulders. And as he slowly made the sign of the cross over the whole congregation, I,

Magister Pietro

facing him and the Host in its gold-radiant house, gravely and gently rocked the censer toward it, making a muted clish-clish that was for the moment the only sound in the sanctuary or the church proper, which I imagined extending up and up, infinitely, into the shadows behind me.

I chose the part for myself by coming early so faithfully, and Father Irish confirmed me in it. Once I had appeared in the sacristy, with the charcoal carefully prepared in the warm censer, he would not give it to anybody else.

But one Sunday night, two weeks after Easter, I had to give it up. When I got to the church Peter DiDonato was leaning against the door of the altar boys' vestry, waiting for me. It was only just dark, nasty and misting out. I could see the white paper, and the hot spark, of his cigarette. I climbed the steps to him.

"Listen Tim, you'll have to tell Father I can't serve tonight."

I never asked him why. Since the part of Thurifer had been conceded to me the year before, he had taken me for granted in it just as I took him for granted as Master. Still, we never talked, and I never really knew him well.

"Okay, sure, Pete."

I looked up. Peter wore a long raincoat, the collar around his ears, no hat. He bowed, a simple bow, thanked me with a look from his grave eyes, went down the steps and walked quickly away.

When I told Father Irish later he didn't ask me anything, either. But his eyebrows rose, his forehead wrinkled and went smooth, and the close-fitting cap of his black hair shrank momentarily.

That Sunday night there weren't many altar boys. Two little sixth graders were given the candles. Father Irish chose a long skinny redhead, a pole vaulter named Joe Grimes, for the Cross. I could see what was coming. I held out the censer to Bob La Fortune, a fat kid two years behind me at school, whose surplice I used to borrow when my own was being washed because he came to serve so seldom, even before I heard his name spoken; and with his smile, and crinkling lines at the corners of his eyes, Father Irish turned to me.

"....and Tim.....Master?"

It was an invitation. I had been on the altar five years. The very first night I served I had been chosen an Acolyte because I was the only other short boy, and I was very much frightened. But I got through it by watching my partner, and afterward Father Irish had bent down and put his hands on my shoulders and said to me, "Wonderful, Tim." Now I looked at him and nodded with the same simple bow that Peter had given me when he left, earlier.

For the next month Peter never came around. He didn't tell me again that he wouldn't be coming and Father didn't say a word about him to me though I was Master through all that time, even to serving on the Epistle side at Sunday high mass.

On the altar things weren't going right. I worried about them all the time. Joe Grimes placed his hands on the cross like a pole vaulter starting for the pit, and I'm ashamed to say how angry I got with Bob La Fortune, but he was so clumsy. The third Sunday, when he tried to lift the censer and *then* raise the lid (instead of the other way around) so that Father Irish could add the incense, he dropped the whole thing — the pot crashed to the floor, the coals and ashes spilled out and the three of us skipped back, to avoid burning our cassocks. It wasn't my fault but I knew that if I had been Thurifer, and Peter DiDonato had been Master, it wouldn't have happened. Everything was screwed up because people weren't playing the parts that were right for them.

I was worried about Peter, too. One morning at school my sister came to me in the hall and said, "Did you hear? Peter DiDonato was in a fight with a man! His hands were all bloody. Gina saw it."

I found Gina Ledbetter. She'd been downtown, waiting for a bus in front of Liggett's, when she heard men's voices yelling "Hey!" and "Hey!" and she turned and there were two men, and at first it looked like they were reaching and slapping each other's faces — she heard slap! slap! slap! — but then one of them had his man's hat fall off and all at once he was down on his hands and knees and she saw how the knuckles of the other, the taller one, had blood all over them and she looked again, and realized it was Peter. Then the bus came and people rushed to get on. The man was hustled away by some other men in hats and Peter went, by himself, back into Liggett's.

I still didn't hear from Peter. I had to figure out the part of Master from the way I had watched him do it for so long, without any help. I'd learned to be Thurifer in the same way; but it was lonely.

I looked in Father Irish's direction. I wondered what he knew, whether he had heard from Peter or tried to get in touch with him. I didn't think so. Father Irish was always just a little remote. He was the friendliest man and everybody liked him, but he was remote. Besides, that wasn't the way it was done on the altar; Peter would come back, or he wouldn't. Father wasn't going to say anything to him.

He didn't say anything to me, either, not about Peter or the way things were going on the altar. Not even after I called Bob La Fortune "Stupid" out loud that Sunday as I picked up the hot coals he'd spilled, with tongs I had to fetch from the vestry. We got the censer back together and finished the service. Father said nothing, Bob La Fortune said nothing, and I said nothing.

It was hard though, and watching Father Irish I wondered if he himself ever got any help at all; or if he, like the rest of us, had to make do with what he had learned from others, watching and remembering.

As for me, I had to know for certain. So I went over to the DiDonatos' house. Gemma answered the door and told me Peter was working with their father as a mason's helper every day after school; but I could come and see him Saturday afternoon.

We sat out on the bungalow's porch in the sun.

"What's going on, Pete?"

"I'm dropping the altar. I'd have to anyway, wouldn't I. Who ever heard of an altar boy that's out of school."

"It's different with you, though."

"Why is it everybody wants me to be a priest," Peter said bitterly, turning away his face. He grunted. "You'd think I didn't like girls as well as anybody." He turned to me again.

"You know what, Tim — you should be the priest. I couldn't even learn to read the Latin. You're smart in school, you could keep up with Father. I never know what he's talking about. Once he said something to me, and the next day Mr. Marcel said the same thing. Shakespeare, or somebody. You know that stuff."

"You and Father can talk in Italian."

"He sings in Italian, but he can't talk it. You should be the priest, Tim." He was quite serious. "You're a lot like Father, even though you might not look it."

"I'm not cut out for it," I said. "I make a terrible Master. I don't think I can do it much longer. Why do you think I came to see you? You have to have a vocation — a call."

"That's a lot of bullshit. You remember that kid, Kevin, Father brought here last fall? We went for a couple of beers. Father gave Kevin the keys to his car. The first thing this Kevin told me was how much the car was worth. Then he told me how much he figured Father gets paid. Father knows how to get good assignments, he said. Some assistants don't even have a car, or their pastors boss them. That was all he talked about. Sure, I was thinking about it — but if that's all there is to it, it isn't for me."

"What are you going to do, then?"

"I'm getting married next month."

He leaned toward me with a fierce, quiet look and all at once I could imagine him winning a fight with a man.

"We have to. Don't look at me like that. You know what I mean."

"Who is it, Pete?"

"Mary Caleski."

"Mary Caleski — but she's a cheerleader! She's the most popular girl in the school. I thought she'd marry some football player."

"Well, I was a football player. That's how I met Mary."

I shook my head. "Oh no, Pete, you know you're not really a football player."

"I'm not? What am I, then?"

I didn't know what to say. I couldn't say he was an altar boy. I couldn't say he was a priest, not yet. I couldn't say he was the Master, or Magister, as Father Irish always called him, and yet that seemed closest to the truth.

"You're just a man," I answered finally. "I mean, nobody would think of you as a kid."

But there again I was wrong. Pete did marry Mary Caleski as soon as they got out of school, and they moved right away into one of those brand new little white houses that Mr. DiDonato, and now his son, were helping to build.

"I never saw anything like it," my own father said, "a boy of eighteen that owns his own house."

My father and my mother had wanted their own house so badly for so long. I was going to say, "He isn't a boy," but I didn't. Because if my father had asked, "What is he, then?" (and he would have), I don't know what I would have answered. I suppose by that time, in the summer, when I had turned seventeen and Peter was living with Mary in their white house, "He's just a man" would have been an honest answer. "In a few years I'll be just a man myself," I might have added.

Because it was at that moment that the thought occurred to me. I was surprised, and at the same time let down. My father too was just a man. There was only one person I knew now who might be different, and that was Father Irish. But I didn't say anything to my father — I had never said anything to him about any of this. By the time school started again, I had dropped the altar myself.

The Washing Machine

The Washing Machine

From the place where he stood, the boy John Sobieski fancied he could make out two cellar indentations in the long shallow hillside, a natural rise in the earth's surface that curved round with the line of lake shore until it met, almost at a right angle, the higher, straighter thrust of the New York Central railroad embankment.

The track had just crossed the river. Here the embankment carried it in a direct line well above the uncertain swampy ground to land it in solid pasture a mile to the west. Far below, the water moved through a great concrete culvert piercing the embankment wall, from the lake out to the nearby river, and in flood season from the river back to the lake again.

He stood out on the ice before high brittle reeds, colorless and absolutely without motion, and looked across from a far low shore. Within the culvert's arch it was dark already; but as to the cellar holes there was enough dry snow, now in mid-December, to bring out the configuration of shapes in the land in black dots and lines — as graphite powder will make clear the contours of fingerprints, or iron filings the lines of force of a magnet.

A wind had swept the milky ice all clear. As the boy stood looking across there he wanted badly, at the same time, to go home. He had just had a painful fall, a fall so hard it seemed he had sprained both wrists. The breath had gone from his stomach for a moment. When finally he picked himself up his ankles would hardly stiffen to steady his skate blades, they were so feeble, he was so weak. He felt all at once how cold and late it really was. As light drained from the air the snow, the lake ice, the remote high sky — clouded in tiny frigid motionless bars — had all begun to glow; by contrast, the solid lines of earth were blackening in with ever more distinct and broader slashes. He was alone. A mile away, at the village end of the lake, skaters had made a yellow-flickering warming fire. And it was just as he had got up, feeling all these things, that he looked across and saw those boldly drawn indentations in the hillside opposite.

"At least I can go home," he thought, and he said aloud, "At least I don't have to stay here."

For a long moment he gazed, shivering, unable to move. A bleak terror was upon him. But then a train crossing the embankment roused him — a thrusting locomotive drawing behind it long rows of yellow lighted windows — clicking across toward Buffalo and the West.

The Washing Machine

It disappeared, but left the rails still ringing behind it.

"At least I don't have to stay here," he said again quietly. But the thought followed, that he did not speak aloud, "What if I did?"

An ache of envy overcame him — of the passengers in those warm yellow cars. They were free by the oldest principle of freedom, free to move over the surface of the inhospitable earth. Earth was no place for men, it was too dangerous and too forgetful. Years before, at this very place, the cellar holes marked it, a woman had died. Two children had died. A man in an access of superhuman strength had lifted a washing machine onto his back, carried it to the water's edge and flung it into the lake.

More than the deaths of twin children of typhoid in this swampy place, or of the mother, a tender young woman wasted by fever and grief, was the memory of that fearful act: the squinting eyes and stiffened faces of the family women, when they spoke of it, reflected fear and grief and awe and even, it seemed, the flickering kerosene light of the scene itself — when the shadowy man, the small railroad worker coming home in the dead of night in his fury, with quick terrible motions, as seen by the indifferent exhausted eyes of his young wife, kicked loose the gasoline tank of the washer, hoisted the machine in the lamplight and then, bent under an incredible crushing burden, nevertheless found his way the few yards down to the lake and threw it off.

For years it remained there — the water wasn't

deep and it had gone in upright — its legs sunk in the mucky bottom, in high water covered, in low water protruding, and all the while rusting, disintegrating, nobody daring to remove it.

It was still there three years afterward when the Sobieskis, in the next house, removed across the river to join other families gathered into substantial two-family houses clustered around St. Stephen's church. God only knew where it was gone by this time — swallowed, absorbed long since by the earth like some bitter but eventually soluble pill.

The small man, the immigrant, had met the young woman on the boat, married her and brought her to live finally in this marginal watery place in a house that was no more than a square shed covering a burrow in the ground. He would leave her with a three-year-old girl and the younger twins while he labored through the day on the railroad. When he saw her burdened and distressed, he brought home the washing machine that would ease her life for her. When still she failed of happiness, he threw the washing machine into the lake.

This man never once looked back. From the lake's edge he did not even return to the house, but mounted the embankment and disappeared down the track.

Two days later the woman and the younger children died. Only the girl remained, to be brought up by steadier people, Sobieskis, who arranged for funerals and burial from St. Stephen's. They took her with them into the city. Very much later she would be married to one of them, and the couple would become the boy's parents.

The tramps who dropped from railroad cars at the threshold of the city resorted to the empty structures below the embankment. Lonely men built fires on the lake shore, consuming the wood of the one while huddling for shelter in the other. In the end the railroad officials had both dismantled, to prevent a jungle growing up.

Such was the story of the washing machine; the boy had known it all his life. By now it almost seemed he could remember seeing it happen himself — in some dark place of his mind lighted by a kerosene lamp turned up full, the flame in two high points like a big yellow tooth, the chimney glass blackening around its narrow top. The look of suffering on the young woman's face it seemed he had known forever. Only the features of the dark figure, author of all this dread, remained obscure, averted from the boy and the young woman both as it carried its intolerable burden: a small and compact figure not staggering, but quick and purposeful.

Under its influence he sat down recklessly on the cold ice. He took off his mittens and undid his skate laces with bare fingers. From the side pockets of his heavy coat he took out shoes and put them on. He knotted the laces and hung the skates around his neck, the blades clicking together in front. In the low cold shoes his feet felt queer and stiff, unnaturally light, unused to walking after skating all afternoon.

He walked just out on the ice underneath last year's pale reeds that stood so high and still — not toward the skating park, with its village and fire, but in the opposite direction. The two shores drew closer together as the lake tapered; the massive culvert, with its dark-filled mouth, rushed out to meet him. Standing beside this cavity he could look across the narrow inlet into the cellar depressions. Snow lay in them. Young trees were growing out of them. Here the ice was blackish, the water moving just underneath, unsafe to cross. Abruptly he turned away and began to climb, at a steep angle, the smooth flank of the railroad. His feet broke through a crust. Snow and cinders seeped into his shoes but at every step, as he rose into the open, clearer air, out of the low marshland where night seemed to gather the sooner, he felt stronger and more relieved. Far over, the floodlights for night skaters at the park came on, and as he reached the top and stepped onto the ties binding the clean, straight rails together, he felt as though he were his own grandfather mounting that same embankment to follow the tracks across the river into the city on the old railroad bridge so many years before.

❖

The Washing Machine

Two hours later he was passing in the cold December dark through the streets around St. Stephen's with its high-pointing Old Country cross and steeple. The houses were lighted inside but all at the back where the kitchens were. In front their faces, their dark window-eyes, were blank. The boy marked the one where he knew his father and mother would be, sitting in an upstairs kitchen, but moved past it on the opposite sidewalk for two long blocks, and turned a corner. On this street the houses were not so compact together, they had wider spaces, and even a vacant lot, in between. He came to a dead end and a street light.

The pavement stopped at a curbing and just beyond, the smooth winter-lines of very young trees ran up-and-down in the circle of light. Outside their sparse barrier was black space and night, the furious rush of air above the river valley. The bluff dropped off steeply to the river flats — and down there even now were five-and six-story factory buildings, and vast sheds of corrugated tin and steel, with streets and bits of track running between; ranks of waiting railroad cars; fields of materiel in wooden crates; trucks and small engines constantly moving; and lights on always through the night, a city in itself, the General Electric Company works: generating a continuous low metallic sound that never ceased, like a warm humming electric motor that is never turned off.

Turning, John Sobieski passed out of the light on his way to the back of the last house. Stuffy and warm as always and tinged with deep ineradicable old smells, the downstairs kitchen received him empty. Upon a heavy round table a fringed lampshade dropped its light. There was an oak sideboard, and a kitchen range with a dozen lids that might be lifted off with a poker. Everything was heavy and dark and old — the curtains and drapes in the other rooms, the overstuffed furniture, the tall parlor stove standing upon claw feet with many sets of doors and fireglass windows all around, scrolls and ledges and fantastic pointing roof shapes as though it were a replica of some high foreign building far away in the Old Country.

An old woman, his father's aunt, who had never married, who lived here with one of the boy's many cousins, came in.

"Johnny — you come to see Dorothy, for a change."

From behind new eyeglasses without rims, her sharp black eyes took him in. Dorothy parted her hair in the middle (as the boy's father still did), pulled it back hard and tied it in a knot behind. "You come here, and sit down." She pulled out the square chair nearest the stove. "I got some good bread for you, I got it this afternoon. My Stevie, he is out somewhere. Out to the grill is where, I bet you." She bustled, moving a kettle from one round stove lid to another. Immediately the water inside began to growl. "Shut up, you," she told it. "Just get hot, here."

"We heard you went away somewhere," she said,

turning back to the boy. "It was in the newspaper, Stevie said. I never read newspapers. Nothing in them, but something to stir you all up."

"I went to New York with the running team. But I got sick. I had to give it up."

He faced the old woman Dorothy frankly, knowing she would miss nothing. A few weeks before it had been terribly important, but now it seemed almost to have happened to somebody else.

"I'm all right now," he told her. "I'll be going back to school after Christmas. I went skating at the lake today. I walked all the way back here — across the old railroad bridge. God, those trains are big up close. They wouldn't ever hit you, but the noise is enough to scare you to death. And the wind, when you're out on that bridge over the river. I was afraid I might fall off."

Looking for praise, he was disappointed; Dorothy poured steaming hot water over a tea bag in a deep mug and set it on the oilcloth in front of him. "Oh, that bridge was always terrible for wind. But we never heard of anybody falling off it."

From the pantry she brought out a round loaf of the Polish bread called *babka*; tucking it under one arm, she cut off thick pieces with a short knife, her strong fist looping the loaf, quivering: the loose hangings of moist bread dropped off like apple peelings. She buttered and pushed them toward him, and the boy ate. He was very hungry, and ever since he had begun running he had craved hot sweet liquids.

The old woman sat down with him. She did not talk, while people she was feeding ate. But she did not watch them closely either, so that the boy, eating and drinking, could glance up and notice her now and then. It was strange how, with some old people he had seen, the flesh seemed to grow whiter and more tender, until in the very old it revealed the delicate blues and reds, the slightest movement of cord and bone underneath; but Dorothy's face had only gone brown, as though baked by heat, for it seemed hard and dry and all its lines and marks, and her eyes themselves, though they remained lively and liquid, tended to black. Her face was large and roughly cut, and he had the notion that if you took away her own and put a man's clothing on her, she would turn into a strong and tough little old man.

"Didn't you use to live down there, Dorothy?" he asked finally.

"Live where. Where you talking about."

"By the lake. On the inlet, under the railroad. I was just down there. I could see where the old houses were."

The old woman got up from the table. "Oh, that was a long time ago, John."

"A long time ago, but it's still the same place."

"Oh yes. Same old place. We don't go there now anymore. Never."

"Why don't you go there, Dorothy?"

"Why should we want to go back there? We were glad to get out. Every one of us, was glad." Dorothy's eyes half closed; she remembered. "That was hard. Hard work. Hard life. Nobody to help you, if you got sick. Nobody to go to."

"What did you do, then?"

"We didn't get sick, boy."

Something struck deep in John Sobieski's chest — like a clock whose secret works have been gathering for just this moment. "Yes, you did. Some people did. They got sick. They died. One night my grandfather came home and threw the washing machine into the lake. My grandmother died. The twins died. My grandfather left and never came back."

The old woman stood before him, her eyes nearly closed in the long squint of recollection. Her face was like a house where the shades are drawn while the inhabitants are preoccupied with some calamity within.

"She was so unhappy."

The voice, so filled with sorrow and distress, caused the boy to reach from his chair to embrace her hard body, her black sweater and dark skirt.

"They never should have lived down there," he cried with a grief he had picked up by contagion, as it were, from living among people infected with it. "Why couldn't they just live in the city, like everybody else?" He could feel the old woman's bones beneath the skirt; she laid a hand on his young head. "Trees are growing out of the cellars," he said.

"She was so unhappy."

"Nobody should have lived there. Why did she stay?"

The old woman freed herself with sudden vigor.

"Why! You're a woman, you live where the man wants. You work hard, your children are sick, you're not happy, what does he care." Dorothy lifted her chin and threw out her chest, she strutted. "He's up in the morning. He's filled with his breakfast. He feels good! The sun is shining! He's big and strong, he works in the air. Hard work, oh yes. Then it's night, he is tired out, but he feels good. He's worked, that's all he cares; he wants hot supper. After, he goes across the bridge to drink. Oh, the man, he is happy!"

"If he was happy, why did he throw out the washing machine."

"Him!" said Dorothy, so fiercely the boy was afraid he had angered her; he asked quickly, "There's two cellar holes. Which one was our house?"

"Your house." The old woman's scorn was annihilating. "Nobody was thinking about you. There was no house, belonged to you."

"My grandfather's house then. The one that threw out the washing machine." Speaking these words the boy John Sobieski experienced a thrill of some kind. For somewhere in his mind he could see, back in a time he wished to recover against the inclination of all those still alive who remembered it, a small black figure detaching itself from a dark horizon, struggling laboriously into view as a man might approach across a wide plain at night when the sky was only less dark and solid in substance than the land on which he walked.

"You should ask your mother," Dorothy said to him.

The Washing Machine   245

"I can't ask her. She would only look at me and cry."

"She was so unhappy."

Once more the old woman's eyes closed in the dream squint, her features became again the mask of grief. The boy felt the same bleak grief in himself, the look on his young face began to resemble the look on hers, for we learn grief as we learn most other things, by imitation; but he exerted his will and actually shook himself, in his chair, as a dog shakes itself free of water.

"Why didn't somebody do something!"

"Why, what would you do?"

"I'd do something." He pressed his jaws so hard together that his teeth hurt.

"Yes, you. You're like your father."

"He's afraid of everything. I'm not like him."

"Yes, you're like him. He knows, what people have to go through. Talk to him."

Outside it was black and late and cold, the darkest week of the year. John Sobieski was glad to pass at last into his own house. They lived upstairs in a gray wooden two-family. It was the only house the boy had known; always, especially since his defeat at New York City, he returned to it with a feeling of "Safe. Now I am in no danger, and without burdens, until once again I step off this porch." But his grandmother and the two children had had no such place and had died.

His father met him in the darkened dining room off the hall, lifted the ice skates from his neck, felt the boy's cold hands with his own, took his coat. He told his father where he had been.

"How could he just leave them? It's so cold. How would you like it, to have to live out there this kind of night?"

"Don't forget — we all lived there once. I was only little, but I remember it."

His father brought him into the front room, used for purposes like writing out a money order for the rent or insurance, or listening for an hour to the tall wooden radio that smelled faintly of furniture polish.

"We were living there before they came. He never had much to do with other people. He came from the Old Country by himself and he kept to himself. He didn't like her going to the city, he thought it made her unhappy. He wanted her to be happy. When he found out he couldn't make her happy no matter how hard he tried, he threw out the washing machine."

"My God — it must have weighed something."

"Oh yes, people still talk about it. Not that anybody saw him do it. There's plenty saw it in the water afterward, though. I've heard of things like it — a man lifting an automobile to save somebody in his family. Or holding up a burning house with his back while they run out."

"But those people were sick — they couldn't run out."

"No," his father said bitterly. "He was the one to run out."

"But what's the matter," the boy cried, grieving once more. "Why do we always fail one another?"

His father consoled him. "We still think of her," he said. "We still think about the both of them."

For a long time the two figures of John Sobieski and his father sat still. They were the same size. They stared at the same spot in the pattern of the living room rug. They might have been listening to the tall radio.

"Did you ever hear what happened to him?" the boy asked suddenly.

"He's dead. He disappeared. That's the kind he was."

"How do you know he's dead? Did you ever hear?"

"O.K. Maybe he isn't dead. Maybe he's alive. Maybe he's got a new family somewhere. Just as if we were dead. Either he's dead or we're dead. It has to be one or the other."

"I've heard that story all my life."

"Listen, those are things nobody can do anything about."

"My grandfather could."

"He could. How do you know."

"I know because he threw out the washing machine."

It seemed to the boy that he saw the figure of his grandfather turned toward him at last; and somehow the figure was saying to him, "Hate sorrow. Hate it. Don't put up with it."

❖

The Washing Machine

The next week at Christmas John Sobieski and his father and his mother all dressed in their best winter clothes and walked in the hard bright midnight up the street to St. Stephen's. After reading the gospel the priest preached a short sermon in English. The old man still had a beautiful tall wave of white hair that made him resemble the blond young men of the neighborhood. But his broad-shouldered chasuble was hung upon a frame of bones; he would die within the year. In a soft voice filled with tender longing he spoke of the story he had just read.

"Never in the Gospels do we read of Bethlehem again. Joseph and Mary went there for the birth of the child, but soon they traveled abroad once more and never returned. So are the newest hopes born in the old, old place. Birth reaches back through long lines of fathers and mothers, and our joy at every new birth is shared by those who have suffered and died before. This is the special meaning of the return to Bethlehem: it brings us in touch with all that has been left behind, all who have been left behind forever."

A need to locate the man who had thrown out the washing machine developed in the young man John Sobieski. It was necessary that his grandfather be brought back to his proper place. Could it be the man still lived somewhere and that memory or instinct might bring him home at last, as creatures are said to seek out some original place before their end. Left behind, the Sobieskis experienced the bitter exasperation of those not given the chance to be heard. John Sobieski learned with surprise that his own father had written long letters to relations and even to churches, in cities in the West; and once, at thirty years of age, he had even traveled by train as far as Chicago seeking the father of the woman he had married.

In a few years John Sobieski would leave himself. He would study elsewhere, and marry and make his life far from the old city and its river. He would take with him the story of the washing machine.

In his work he traveled a good deal. He went to St. Louis, Chicago, Milwaukee. He walked the rundown streets of great wooden towns, streets much like those he had known around St. Stephen's. Once, near the end of such a street, in sight of a low factory building served by a disused railroad line where houses had already been pulled out here and there like bad teeth, he found a notice-board attached to the weathering clapboards of a two-family house. The weeds in a small front yard were as high as his chest but he moved into them to look more closely at the writing and drawing, in faded pencil, on sheets that had been through the rains many times. "The Three Greatest Mathematical Problems of All Time Solved. The Trisection of the Angle. The Square of the Circle. The Duplication of the Cube." In some obscure way he took it for a sign of his vanished grandfather, a cryptic message like the one left behind by the lost Roanoke colonists.

The Washing Machine

But his own search, like his father's, came to nothing. The truth was that every effort to recover the man must be circular, turning back on itself only to inspire some new vain attempt. Leaving, he had doomed those behind to such fruitless effort until they should arrive at some pitch of exasperation that would match his own, at the moment when he threw out the washing machine. Only then could they free themselves of him as he had freed himself of them. It must be taken as certain that he had another family somewhere, which had no care for them because it did not know of them. Even if he were living, what could he know of John Sobieski's mother and father, not to speak of John Sobieski himself. Nothing but family memory connected them, and that ran in one direction only. That powerful small man, acting in a confusion of kerosene light against a dark Old Country background, was gone once and for all.

Still later, as a young husband and father, John Sobieski wondered would he tell his own children the story of the washing machine. Grief had to stop somewhere, he reflected. It was not life, a flame to be nourished. He decided that he would not.